Also by Polly Horvath

The Pepins and Their Problems
with pictures by Marylin Hafner

The Canning Season

Everything on a Waffle

The Trolls

When the Circus Came to Town

The Happy Yellow Car

No More Cornflakes

An Occasional Cow
with pictures by Gioia Fiammenghi

The Corps of the Bare-Boned Plane

The VACATION

The
VACATION

★ POLLY HORVATH ★

SQUARE
FISH

Farrar Straus Giroux

NEW YORK

SQUARE
FISH
An Imprint of Macmillan
175 Fifth Avenue
New York, NY 10010
mackids.com

THE VACATION. Copyright © 2005 by Polly Horvath.
All rights reserved. Printed in the United States of America by
R. R. Donnelley & Sons Company, Harrisonburg, Virginia.

Square Fish and the Square Fish logo are trademarks of Macmillan and
are used by Farrar Straus Giroux under license from Macmillan.

Square Fish books may be purchased for business or promotional use. For information on bulk
purchases, please contact the Macmillan Corporate and Premium Sales Department at
(800) 221-7945 x5442 or by e-mail at specialmarkets@macmillan.com.

Library of Congress Cataloging-in-Publication Data
Horvath, Polly.
  The vacation / Polly Horvath.
    p. cm.
  Summary: When his parents go to Africa to work as missionaries, twelve-year-old
Henry's eccentric aunts, Pigg and Mag, take him on a cross-country car trip,
allowing him to gain insight into his family and himself.
  ISBN 978-1-250-06279-6 (paperback) / 978-1-4668-6302-6 (ebook)
  [1. Vacations—Fiction. 2. Aunts—Fiction. 3. Family problems—Fiction.
4. Interpersonal relations—Fiction. 5. Self-perception—Fiction. 6. Automobile
travel—Fiction.] I. Title.

PZ7.H7922Vac 2005
[Fic]—dc22

                                                    2004057667

Originally published in the United States by Farrar Straus Giroux
First Square Fish Edition: 2015
Book designed by Jay Colvin
Square Fish logo designed by Filomena Tuosto

10 9 8 7 6 5 4 3 2 1

AR: 5.6 / LEXILE: 1040L

To Arnie, Emmy, Becca, Keena, and Zayda

Contents

A Little History

I WAS ON WEEK TWO of living with Aunt Magnolia and Aunt Pigg. There was a whole river not that far from us in Critz, Virginia, named after Ralston Pigg, the Daniel Boone of our family, and when my aunt was born, my grandmother gave her the name Pigg, too. My father took me to see the Pigg River once even though the Piggs were my mother's ancestors. We watched its mini majesty (it wasn't a very big river) crashing over rocks, and he said it looked nothing like my aunt, and laughed. Then he said, "Seriously, Henry, if you ever get a chance to name a river, don't name it something like Pigg. Rivers are too important. They're part of a whole water structure that supports life, if you think about it. Think about it!" he suddenly demanded. He worked for the Filmore Brush Company in sales and was usually on the road, but when he was home, he tried to tell me as much about life as he could, to keep me safe when he couldn't be with me. "Once you become a parent, that's the only thing you really want for the rest of your life," he said, his hand resting on my shoulder. "For your children to be safe forever. Even when you can't be with them." He turned to me then and gave me a steely wide-eyed look. "Don't die," he ordered.

The week after I turned twelve, my mother decided to go to Africa as a missionary. She wasn't religious, at least as far as my father and I knew. I heard her telling my father about her plan on the phone. She said she thought her best bet was to be a Mormon because we had Mormon friends and so my mother knew that Mormons were supposed to spend some time on a missionary journey. My mother was trying to convince my father to become Mormon with her, but he didn't want to. And he did not want to go to Africa on a mission with her. He really liked the Filmore Brush Company. He liked being on the road. I heard my mom arguing with him about it a lot because she forgot to keep her voice down, and even when she didn't, our house, although old, had thin walls, and I, the only child, was used to creeping around corners, listening in on my mother's phone conversations. She had a lot of phone conversations because my father was gone so much and I think she liked chatting. I thought she might have dreamt up all this Mormon missionary stuff to bring my father home, although that wasn't what she was like at all, and besides, when he did come home all they did was fight.

"I don't wish to be known as Norman the Mormon," said my father when he got home from one of his business trips.

"I don't think that is inevitable," said my mother. "I'm sure they'll just call you Norman like everyone else. Maybe Norm."

"It's disrespectful to pretend to be religious when we're not. Just so you can get a free trip to Africa."

That one caused slammed doors and three days of silent meals. They didn't think I knew what was going on, and they didn't seem to care how horrible it was for me when they fought. I walked around with nervous tension in my stomach. When I wasn't worried about that, I worried a lot about leaving Virginia for Africa, but I was even more horrified when they told me that I wasn't going to Africa with them.

"We can't possibly take you, Henry," said my mother.

"Too many things could go wrong," said my father.

"There's diseases there you can't even spell."

"And dangerous animals and things in the water, both microscopic and huge."

"Animal and insect and germ things."

"It's no place to take a child."

"And I can't concentrate on missionary work if you're

there," said my mother. "I'll be too busy making sure no harm comes to you."

"I can watch over myself," I offered.

"Not in Africa."

"You'll be with Aunt Magnolia and Aunt Pigg for a few months," said my father.

"Is that how long you'll be gone?" I asked querulously because that was a long time and certainly longer than I wanted to spend with Aunt Magnolia and Aunt Pigg.

"It depends," said my mother, getting a dreamy look in her eye. "It might be longer. I might turn out to be good at this."

"At missionary work!" my father snorted. "I told you to forget all that nonsense."

"Well, how am I supposed to finish out my school year?" I asked. "It's my last year at Critz Elementary. I can't believe you're making me move to Floyd and miss the last weeks at Critz."

"We thought of that. Aunt Pigg and Aunt Magnolia have graciously agreed to move here while you finish school, and then during the summer months you will move back up there to stay with them in Floyd."

"You're going to be gone *summertime*, too?" I wailed as the realization hit me. I could hardly believe this was happening. And Floyd in the summer? What about baseball? I played baseball all summer long in the field by our house. It was the best part of any summer.

"We might be," said my mother. "You never can tell."

"You can tell," said my father. "I told the Filmore Brush Company I would be back by July." He looked at me meaningly. I knew he thought this whole thing was a great indulgence, and was hoping it would settle my mother down for the next ten or fifteen years. Later, in a man-to-man talk, he told me that women could become terribly flighty in middle age. It was best to hook them when they were young and leave them before it started happening. But the thing was, he said, by that time, if you loved them, well, you were stuck.

"I think it's important we have these talks now," he said, patting my shoulder, "just in case."

"In case of *what*?" I asked.

"In case one of those things that happen to people in Africa happens to us. One of those bad things. Those disease things, or light aircraft things, or bad drinking water things. Or large animal things. There's no point pretending that people aren't worried about these things, and the reason they worry is that they're *really, really dangerous*. But I believe you should be clear about the danger before we go. Although, realistically speaking, we'll probably come back just fine with a lot of swell photos."

"Well, I hope so," I said.

"We *all* hope so," said my father. "Except perhaps your mother, who, I think, is looking forward to the dangerous part the most."

"Isn't there anyone who could stay with me besides Aunt Magnolia and Aunt Pigg?" I asked.

"What's wrong with Magnolia and Pigg?" asked my father in surprise, and really, it was kind of hard to put your finger on.

Aunt Magnolia and Aunt Pigg came into town for holiday meals and only stayed a couple of hours. A lot of the time was spent outside our house because they both smoked and Mom wouldn't let them smoke in the house. And they didn't talk to me. I don't think they liked children. Maybe they just didn't like boys. They were extremely adult adults with no play in them. I was always excused immediately after family meals to go watch television. I think they somehow made my mother feel ashamed of me. As if my table manners weren't quite right, or I wasn't quite smart enough, or my conversation, which was nonexistent when they were around, wasn't quite up to par.

"I just wish someone was staying with me who liked me a little more," I said.

"Good opportunity for them to get to know you," said my father, patting my shoulder again absently as if he had already moved on in his head. Heart-to-heart completed, and now he was worrying about the packing or something. "And for you to get to know them!" he added suddenly, a bonus thought.

So my mother went ahead with her plans for Africa, although it turned out that she couldn't become a Mormon missionary on such short notice. The Church said they were sorry about that but hoped she would still think about becoming Mormon while in Africa, should she end up going anyway. One of my mother's contacts at the Mustard Seed, the homeless shelter where she volunteered, offered to write to someone he knew who was helping to build a school in Africa. He thought they would welcome a couple more pairs of hands. I think my my mom was hoping for free accommodations and food. She needed to feel the trip had a purpose that was nobler than making my father do what *she* wanted to do for a change. At least that's how it seemed to me. Maybe I was being unfair. But she did let my father know that she planned to tell everyone she was a Mormon missionary anyway.

"You mean you're going to lie? About something like that?" asked my father. He was becoming more and more perturbed about my mother, who had never broken out in this way before.

"It will open doors," said my mother.

"I'm not going to lie," said my father. "I think that's just nuts."

I didn't know where all this would lead them. I thought my father might even cancel the trip. I couldn't believe that he was going to go along to Africa with her under those circumstances, but he did.

The Flu

AFTER MY AUNTS CAME, I moved into my closet to get as far away from them as I could. Not that they ever came looking for me that first week. I moved a small battery-operated light into it, and some pillows and blankets and a stack of books, and I closed the door and tried to pretend my aunts didn't exist, while they were downstairs ignoring me. I didn't even know that they knew that's where I was until the second week.

"Henry! Come out of the closet," yelled Aunt Pigg from the bottom of the stairs. Aunt Pigg could not bear sleeping upstairs in the spare room or my parents' bedroom. It was too close to the sound of my breathing. She never said this exactly, but it was what I was able to surmise. So she slept in the basement on our rec room sofa. I learned a lot about Aunt Pigg's and Aunt Magnolia's pecking order that first week. Aunt Magnolia got first pick of everything. First pick of the TV shows. First pick of what they made for dinner. First pick of the best place to sleep. If you discounted the upstairs rooms, then the best place to sleep was on the living room couch because the living room was air-conditioned, unlike the rec room, where Aunt Pigg ended up. The whole of the South was having an especially hot spring. Temperatures rose early and high. Our basement should have been air-conditioned, but the air-conditioning system, my father had explained to me, had been a lemon. "Son," he said, "many of the things you are going to buy in your life are going to be lemons. There is nothing you can do about this. Do not blame yourself. Do not blame your spouse. Try not to blame each other."

"Can you blame the company you bought it from?" I asked.

"Not always," he said. My father was a fair man.

Except for the air-conditioning, which was of prime importance, the rec room was more desirable. It had its own bathroom, there was a television down there, and a pool table if Aunt Pigg cared for a little midnight game of pool. It was certainly more private than Aunt Magnolia's living room couch, where anyone who came to the door could see how she slept, the covers all messed up every-where, the empty cracker boxes lying about, or the spilled Coke. Not that there were these things initially. Aunt Magnolia was very neat until she got the flu. That's why

Aunt Pigg was calling me downstairs. I really did not see what I could do about it, although I was sympathetic. I could hear Aunt Magnolia throwing up in the bathroom.

"She's terribly, terribly sick, and I'm worried," said Aunt Pigg, pacing around and wringing her hands. "Magnolia thinks it's a result of quitting smoking, but surely not? I quit smoking before we came, too. We thought it was a good opportunity, since your mother won't let us smoke in the house, but *I'm* not throwing up. I think it's time we called your parents' doctor. Do you know his name?"

I tried to give her the name of my own doctor, but she said that Aunt Magnolia couldn't be seen by a pediatrician. Even I must know *that*. She must have been very worried about Aunt Magnolia because, although distant and not familially welcoming, my aunts were never intentionally unpleasant. Later I found out I simply hadn't known them well enough to know just how unpleasant they could be.

"I get the flu all the time," I said to Aunt Pigg. In elementary school people throw up a lot. My mother said that she went many grownup years never throwing up, but as soon as I started going to elementary school and bringing home germs, everyone in the family began throwing up. "When you're around elementary school children, you get used to it."

"Well, nevertheless, boy, we must do something for

her," said Aunt Pigg. "If you can't tell me your parents' doctor's name, I will have to go through your father's desk and try to find it."

"I don't think he keeps things like that in his desk," I said. Which was true. Mostly he kept brushes. He got a lot of brush samples, and he had them neatly labeled with all the things they would and wouldn't do. After all, he was a brush representative; what else should he have in his desk?

"He must have it under a list of names in his computer, then," said Aunt Pigg.

"I wouldn't know," I said finally, and left for school because I had no more helpful suggestions.

When I got home, Aunt Pigg and Aunt Magnolia weren't there, so I gathered they had gone to a doctor after all. It was pleasant to have an afternoon where I didn't feel I had to stay in the closet to have a little peace. Around suppertime I heard them come in. Aunt Magnolia certainly looked very green. She was slumped against Aunt Pigg's shoulder and moaning loudly.

"Ayeee, ayeee," she said over and over and then went into the bathroom to throw up. I did feel sorry for her. I knew it was a terrible thing to be that sick.

"Would you like me to make you some tea?" I asked because my mother had taught me how. You put water in the electric kettle, flip the switch, and then when it stops boiling, you pour it over a tea bag. I had not known at the time what I would be able to do with this skill, but here I was, able to offer Aunt Magnolia some solace.

"Please go away, little boy," said Aunt Magnolia.

"She's delirious," whispered Aunt Pigg, helping Aunt Magnolia to her couch. I didn't believe that Aunt Magnolia was delirious. I think she had just grabbed that opportunity to be rude under cover of delirium, but I didn't mind. When you're that sick you must take what joy comes your way.

Aunt Magnolia was sick for two weeks, during which time the house was fairly quiet and I got a great deal of reading done in my closet. But by the fourth week of their stay, Aunt Pigg got restless. So did Aunt Magnolia, who was weakened greatly and living on dry toast and crackers. I could have provided tea, but I hid the tea bags out of spite because she'd been so rude. I had heard her talking to Aunt Pigg about how short I was for my age, which I'm not. Not *that* short. And how I was neurotic because I spent all my time in my closet. And how being an only child had probably warped me and about how it was all my mother's fault, pretending to be a Mormon missionary.

"What do you suppose he *does* in there, hour after hour?" asked Aunt Magnolia.

"Do you want to go check?" said Aunt Pigg.

"Yes. Let's!"

I ran out of the closet and into my parents' bathroom and locked the door. After that I moved pillows and blankets into my parents' bathtub and called it my bunker. I retired there whenever I heard them coming upstairs. It didn't become a game exactly, more an unspoken meanness on both sides.

"He's not here anymore," I heard Aunt Pigg whisper as they tiptoed out of my closet.

"He runs when he hears us coming," whispered Aunt Magnolia.

"If you could just try climbing the stairs faster . . ." suggested Aunt Pigg.

"For heaven's sakes, I'm sick, Pigg. And I'm becoming sooooo bored," whined Aunt Magnolia. "So dreadfully, dreadfully bored."

"So am I," said Aunt Pigg.

"Let's rearrange all Katherine's furniture," said Aunt Magnolia.

And so they did.

• • •

Although it sounds strange, the rearranging of the furniture was a natural diversion because they owned and ran an interior decorating company called Pigg Designs. I thought that was a terrible name, but no one else I knew ever commented on it. It was the reason they were able to come and stay with me. It was a very profitable company and made a lot of money, so when the time came, they were able to leave it with their assistants, drop everything, and embrace their family duties with open arms.

"Always have some family around for when you need a family duty embraced," my father said to me. "Give them an occasional holiday meal, ignore their profligate smoking or cussing or soap opera fixation or whatever it is about them that you despise, and never forget their birthdays." At the time I thought it was a lot to go through for an occasional favor. Later I was glad.

Aunt Magnolia was still terribly, terribly weak and she would lie on the couch in the center of the living room, where she still slept amidst the chaos, and point, and Aunt Pigg would carry out her ideas. They started by rearranging furniture, but it quickly got out of control and they decided to repaint the entire house burnt orange. Furniture was piled up in the centers of rooms. Aunt Pigg had hired some brawny college boys to come in and move things around as needed, but she was doing all the painting herself. "The thing is to *keep busy*." She would nervously hiss things like this in my ear. I think she was talking as much to herself as to me because she was more worried about Aunt Magnolia than she was willing to admit. But it was unnerving to have her always coming up and clutching my upper arm and hissing things at me when I got home from school. Even though I'd come to expect it, every time she sidled over and suddenly grabbed me, it scared the bejesus out of me.

Aunt Pigg asked me if I thought my mother would like the color. I was reasonably sure she would hate burnt orange, but on the other hand, I thought, that's what you get for becoming a fake Mormon missionary. I felt sorry for my father, though. None of this was his fault, but it was being visited on him anyway.

"Just please leave my closet alone," I said.

"Oh, I don't think we could do that," said Aunt Pigg, looking shocked at the idea, and slapping on a nicotine patch. "But don't worry. We aren't painting any of the closets burnt orange."

"Ah," I said. I didn't want to engage her in decorating talk, so I said as little as possible.

"We're painting them steel blue."

"With burnt orange?" I couldn't help squawking.

"Exactly, boy, exactly. I'm glad to see you have an eye for color. Most boys your age wouldn't think of it one way or another. Burnt orange and steel blue, not a good combination, right?"

"No!" I croaked.

"But wait and see. Wait and see!" said Aunt Pigg, tapping her nose with her finger. I kept staring at her because I wasn't sure what the nose tapping meant, and then I realized what had troubled me all along. Aunt Pigg really did have a nose like a pig's. It was short and turned up and there was a good inch of space or so between it and her naturally upturned lips. I had been avoiding looking her full in the face, but now I realized that if you ran across her on a dark street, you would probably cross to the other side. It was the mouth always smiling even when she wasn't, like the Joker in Batman.

• • •

And so I lost my closet as the painting progressed.

"You're not going to paint the bathrooms, are you?" I asked from the bathtub.

"Well, eventually something will have to be done with them," said Aunt Magnolia thoughtfully. She had dragged herself upstairs. She was dragging herself all over the house to help with things even though anyone could see she was still terribly sick. She might not be throwing up anymore, but she was as thin as a rail and sporting big ugly bruises everywhere and her gums kept bleeding, so she often had a little trail of blood going down her chin before she caught it. It was really as if she was oozing to death, if that's possible. She reminded me of a banana that's been kept too long. I expected fruit flies to begin gathering in her hair. I was afraid to touch her because I thought she would be unbearably squishy beneath the skin. "*Please* lie down, Aunt Magnolia," I said to her every time I passed her. I thought it was the least I could do. In my letters to my father I wrote, Please tell Aunt Magnolia to lie down. But the letters took so long to get to Africa that it turned out to be a worthless way to communicate. I didn't get a response before *it* happened.

"Well, now it's happened," said Aunt Magnolia one day, tearing open a telegram from my father.

What it was, was that my father had lost my mother. My mother had gotten tired of pretending to be a Mormon missionary. She and my father were helping to build a school, which she did cheerfully as if she were a missionary, although she couldn't think of anything inspirational to say to anyone, and then she got interested in the chimps in Uganda after talking to some primatologists who were wandering through, so suddenly she wanted to leave Kenya to go to Uganda and join up with a tour who got to watch a team of primatologists who were tracking chimps. Everyone kept telling my parents that it was usually the reverse. People got assigned to Uganda and couldn't wait to get their rear ends to Kenya, but my mother never was like anyone else. So they went to have a little Ugandan holiday and were taken to see some chimps with a bunch of other tourists, and one minute she was there, and the next, one of the student primatologists and my mother had headed off suddenly after a chimp and never came back. The other primatologists said not to worry, that the student who disappeared with my mother had been known to go off suddenly like this and so far had always made it back in one piece, but my father was still understandably concerned. My father asked the guide who had arranged the meeting with the chimp watchers what he thought about it.

"It's never good when people disappear in Africa," said the guide.

"Serves her right. Oh dear," said Aunt Magnolia, lying on the couch and reading the telegram twice. "That's a very long telegram. It must have cost him a fortune. I wonder why he didn't just phone? Well, this is no good, is it, Pigg?"

"I told Katherine she shouldn't go to Africa," said Aunt Pigg. "But perhaps she will be okay."

"*What do you mean, perhaps?*" I shouted. I'd had just about enough of this cavalier attitude toward my mother.

"Oh, Katherine's always been excellent at caring for herself and others. She's probably forgotten all about your father and the tour and is tending to sick monkeys and helping the student chart unknown monkey behavior," said Aunt Magnolia.

"Forgotten my father!" I shouted. I was so incensed that I went to the bathroom and locked myself in until breakfast. The truth is, my mother is a bit like that. She is always giving her full attention to whoever she is with at the time, so that if you aren't with her, it feels very out of sight, out of mind. But the thing is that when you *are* with her, well, she is *really* with you and you feel enveloped by her goodness and wonder why you ever felt abandoned. And then as soon as you are away from her, it's as if you could disappear forever and that would be okay, too. My mother calls it not being attached and it's as far away from my father's way of being as can be, but I think it stems from my mother's belief that we are all okay every minute and always will be no matter what, but sometimes it feels like it would be nice if she worried about you or needed to see *you*, and she never seems to. You have to go to her; she just doesn't seem to have those needs. It can drive people crazy, that kind of love.

Later, Aunt Pigg made banana waffles for breakfast, which I suppose was a sort of apology for who they were by nature, the kind of women who say it serves her right before they even start worrying. But by breakfast they were pretty worried about her, which made me feel much better, although not as good as I would have felt to find them both throwing up their waffles all over everything. I was still pretty mad.

When I got home from school, Aunt Pigg assaulted me. "There is *hope!*" she said.

"Specifics, Pigg," said Aunt Magnolia.

She handed a telegram to me. It was from my father. It read: "Two people in same-colored clothes as Katherine and student spotted in jungle by tourists. Sure are fine. Just lost. Perhaps Katherine enjoying pretending to be Jane Goodall. Will keep you informed. Not to worry."

So that was that temporarily, and my aunts went back to decorating and I gave up trying to write my parents, since they were both preoccupied.

Magnolia Sickens

"OH, PIGG, OH, PIGG, I feel my light fading." Aunt Magnolia lay on the couch and pointed out spots on the trim that Aunt Pigg had missed. It was an ugly steel blue, but it didn't look bad with the burnt orange, just as Pigg had predicted. If people are going to take it upon themselves to redecorate your house, it is as well that they are working professionals.

Aunt Magnolia was sickening. Even I could tell. Aunt Pigg was deep in denial. She kept talking Aunt Magnolia out of going to the doctor until the house was finished. If Aunt Magnolia went into the hospital, Aunt Pigg would have to finish the job alone.

"Now we just have to pick out some fabric swatches," said Aunt Pigg, holding a sheaf of them up in front of Aunt Magnolia's misted eyes.

"I think this one," said Aunt Magnolia, getting interested. She would always perk up when there was a choice to be made. It's probably what led her into decorating to begin with.

"Oh, not that one, surely," said Aunt Pigg. "I don't think it goes with the orange at all. Bright orange with burnt orange?"

"You're not re-covering the couches, are you?" I asked. I had been sitting at the kitchen table having cookies and milk after school and peering in through the dining room archway, spying on the decorating. We had one of those big open floor plans that allowed me to see what they were up to without having to actually *be* with them.

"What's that? What's that sound?" asked Aunt Magnolia, the back of her hand resting ever so lightly on her fevered forehead. "Is there a neighbor loose?"

"No, that's *Henry*," said Aunt Pigg, "the little boy that Katherine had. He's twelve years old. He *lives* with us."

"I *know* who Henry is, Pigg," said Aunt Magnolia in exasperation.

"I was just practicing," said Aunt Pigg, unperturbed.

"Practicing for *what*?" snapped Aunt Magnolia.

"The day," said Aunt Pigg, and then stopped tactfully. She had told me that she believed Aunt Magnolia's demise would soon reach her brain and we'd be tying a bib around her at mealtimes and trying to spoon soggy Wheaties into her.

"What does he want anyway?" asked Aunt Magnolia crankily. She had said she didn't mind the idea of sliding into a ladylike demise but it irritated her that anyone would ever think she could lose her mental faculties. There was nothing romantic about that *at all*.

"He is worried about the couches. He doesn't like the fabric swatch you picked either," Aunt Pigg elaborated fictitiously.

"Well, tell him to go to the Rhode Island School of Design if he's so smart. Bright orange it is. That was the perfect swatch, Pigg."

"Mother won't like her couches being re-covered," I said boldly.

"How would you know?" asked Aunt Pigg.

"Because I know my mother," I said.

"Did anything in your upbringing lead you to believe she would someday pretend to be a Mormon missionary?" asked Aunt Magnolia unfairly.

I sat in dignified if sulky silence.

"Well then," said Aunt Magnolia smugly, "we're doing our dear Katherine a favor while she has her little African holiday."

"Stop that," I said, and went upstairs to sit in the bathtub. In spite of the bunch of sheets and blankets and pillows in there, it still wasn't very comfortable. I much preferred my closet, but it was covered in steel blue wet paint. Every time I thought it was dry, Pigg would put another coat on. Things were becoming intolerable. And then they started pulling out the kitchen cabinets.

Because the kitchen was being remodeled and there was plaster dust everywhere, we had to eat all our meals out. Breakfast had become juice boxes and granola bars, and I took my lunch to school anyway. But every night we sort of heaved drooping Aunt Magnolia into the car, bruises and all, and carted her to some restaurant. In Critz, there is not a lot of choice of where to eat. The first night we went to Captain Sam's. The second night we went to the Main Street Bakery and Café. The third night we went to Captain Sam's.

"All the shrimp you can eat," said the waitress, coming up to us.

"You said that last time," said Aunt Magnolia sullenly.

"Oh," said the waitress, and looked crushed. I felt sorry for her. She was probably another Critz high school dropout trying to make her way in a pleasant manner through what she would discover was an unforgiving world. "Didn't you get all the shrimp you could eat?"

"That is neither here nor there," answered Aunt Magnolia. "In point of fact, I ordered the king crab."

"Did you get enough of that?" asked the waitress in a kind of desperate hopelessness.

"That's neither here nor there either because the king crab was not an all-you-can-eat special, do correct me if I am wrong."

"You're right," said the waitress miserably. She was being corrected an awful lot during this wretched encounter.

"Although no one could have gotten enough crab because it took about ten minutes to free a tiny morsel from the shell. I got enough shell, though; does that count? Miles of giant shell legs sticking out at all angles, sticking me, making my gums bleed."

The waitress couldn't help it, she stared at Aunt Magnolia's gums, which were still bleeding. There was a thin line of blood always pooling in the corner of her mouth.

"You ought to see a doctor about that," said the waitress. "I had an Uncle Norm with gum disease and his gums bled just like that. Maybe not a doctor, now that I think about it. Maybe a dentist." She brightened up for a moment, pleased with herself for contributing, in no matter how small a way, to Aunt Magnolia's well-being.

"I'd really rather just have dinner," said Aunt Magnolia, who was taking no prisoners.

"What can I get you now?" whispered the waitress. She was obviously afraid to speak, but she had to take our order.

"How about menus?" said Aunt Magnolia coolly. "Or are you planning instead on just tossing shrimp out the kitchen door at us? All the shrimp you can catch?" Then Aunt Magnolia gave a kind of sudden snort of laughter. I think she surprised herself by making a joke even she thought was funny. The waitress winced.

"I'll get you menus," said the girl and fairly ran for the hostess station, where we could see her pointing us out to the hostess. We were given another waitress after that.

"You know," said Aunt Pigg on the way home in the car, "I know you aren't feeling well, but I don't think you should take it out on the waitress."

"I need to find a decent doctor!" shouted Aunt Magnolia. "And I don't have the energy to do it. You have to find one for me, and not that awful one I saw last time. He didn't know anything."

"As soon as we finish the kitchen," said Aunt Pigg imperturbably. "You know it's just the flu, Mag. He told you so."

"I don't believe it," croaked Aunt Magnolia.

"You did want to pick the fabric for re-covering the kitchen chairs and curtains, didn't you? I was thinking gingham."

"Not gingham, Pigg, tell me you didn't say gingham," said Aunt Magnolia, turning to face her, her attention immediately diverted.

"A nice pink or yellow perhaps."

"Oh, Pigg, have I taught you nothing?"

The Birthday Party

FOR TWO WEEKS Aunt Pigg and Aunt Magnolia worked on the kitchen. The college guys came and went, came and went. Aunt Pigg kept saying, "In the kitchen the college boys come and go, talking of Michelangelo." But they weren't. They were generally talking about the Oakland Raiders and the Tampa Bay Buccaneers. When they weren't grunting. Some of that kitchen equipment was pretty heavy. As much as Aunt Pigg and Aunt Magnolia had a keen eye for decorating, they had no eye at all for landscaping, because whenever a college boy would ask where a discarded cabinet or appliance should go, Aunt Pigg would say, "Ummm, just . . ." and she'd point for them to toss it on a growing pile in the middle of our smallish backyard.

"I think the neighbors are going to complain," I said.

"Why ever should they?" asked Pigg. "Your backyard is so big nobody will even notice."

"It is not. It's a small backyard and it's covered in junk," I contested hotly.

"It's much bigger than Mag's and my backyard. You don't know a small backyard until you've seen ours. Now, that's small, honey," said Aunt Pigg. Because she called me "honey" instead of "boy," for a moment I thought she was warming to me, and then I remembered that she called the college boys "honey," too. "You know, I'm glad your mother called us to take care of you."

"You are?" I asked in surprise.

"Why, yes," said Aunt Pigg. "Magnolia and I have never had carte blanche to do the whole of someone's house without interference. There's a cohesiveness about it that is very satisfying, don't you think?"

I spent the next couple of days in the bathtub. I refused to be part of the cohesiveness. But they didn't seem to notice because, as it turned out, Magnolia's fortieth birthday was approaching. We were eating at Captain Sam's when Aunt Magnolia pointed this out.

"I refuse to have my birthday dinner at Captain Sam's, so the kitchen has to be ready in three days, Pigg," said Aunt Magnolia. She was lying slumped in the booth, her head just appearing over the table. We had stopped having dinner at the Main Street Bakery and Café because they had only metal chairs and Aunt Magnolia found it hard to remain completely upright in one all through dinner. "If I make it to my birthday."

"I told you, the new cabinets go in tomorrow and then, knock wood, we're done," said Pigg happily. She had finally succumbed to the all-you-can-eat shrimp, once she found out she could order them broiled, no butter, and was forking them down with wild abandon. "More shrimp!" she would call gaily every time a waitress came out of the kitchen. The staff was now flipping coins to see who would get stuck waiting on us. "More shrimp over here, please! Oh, perk up, Mag, you'll probably outlive all of us!" She didn't care about anything when she was knocking back crustaceans.

But Aunt Magnolia almost didn't. The morning of her birthday I got to sleep in because it was a professional development day and no school. I'd had breakfast in the kitchen because Aunt Pigg had completed it as promised, and was making my way to the downstairs bathroom when I ran into Aunt Magnolia, rounding the corner, doing the same.

"Might as well see how the face of forty looks," she muttered, turning toward me. I took one look and made an involuntary sound of horror.

"Very funny," she said.

But it wasn't. Sometime in the night her lip must have caught on a tooth and bled all over her face. There was blood caked on the lip and all over her chin and cheeks, where it had dried during the night. Her hair was stuck in it. Her face was almost white and she had huge smudges under her eyes and a bruise on her neck. If anyone looked close to death, it was Aunt Magnolia.

Aunt Pigg, who came running when I yelped, took one look at Aunt Magnolia and said, "Oh, Mag, we'd better find you a new doctor."

Aunt Pigg found a doctor in the yellow pages who would see Aunt Magnolia, and we drove over.

The nurse took one look at Aunt Magnolia and made the same involuntary sound of alarm. "I told her we should have washed the blood off before coming," said Aunt Pigg, picking up a magazine and sitting down again while the nurse took Aunt Magnolia into the examining room. The doctor sent Aunt Magnolia for tests and we squired her about from place to place and finally home, where we waited for the doctor to call with the results that afternoon. It turned out that Aunt Magnolia had something called idiopathic thrombocytopenia purpura. When Aunt Pigg and I first heard this, we gasped and thought she was a goner for sure. But it turned out that all it meant was that her body, in a sort of hyper-responsible way, was killing off everything, not just germs but its own blood platelets, too. That's why she was bleeding.

"Some birthday present," said Aunt Magnolia glumly after the doctor called.

"At least you can eat again," said Aunt Pigg. "You can have some lovely chocolate birthday cake."

"Don't want any," said Aunt Magnolia, lying on the couch. "I'm just going to lie here and bleed."

"Well, almost anything would improve the color of those slipcovers," said Aunt Pigg. She let Aunt Magnolia pick all the fabrics to keep her interested in the project and then complained about her choices constantly afterward.

"Well, happy fortieth," I said.

It was apparently the wrong thing to say because Aunt Magnolia snarled, "I wonder how your mother, the monkey lady, is doing?"

I did not wish her happy birthday again.

At dinner we took a festive tray to her, but she claimed to be too ill to eat. A neighbor brought over a budding hyacinth, which smelled wonderful. Like spring. And asked Aunt Pigg to please have all the trash off the lawn by Monday or she would have to call the authorities.

Aunt Pigg put the hyacinth on a table next to Aunt Magnolia, who pretended to ignore it, but every time I tiptoed through the living room I saw Aunt Magnolia's nose surreptitiously stuck in it. She would breathe it in, great gulps of life-giving, flowerful air, before sinking into her bed of gloom.

"Oh, doom, Henry," she would moan if she happened to see me pass through. "Oh, doom."

Aunt Magnolia's Idea

FORTUNATELY, as the days went on, Aunt Magnolia's platelet test showed that she was on the rebound and her body had stopped all its indiscriminate destruction. We began to find her lying on the couch with a steely look of speculation in her eye. I, for one, did not like it and I could tell it was making Aunt Pigg nervous. It shifted the dynamics in the house. Instead of Aunt Pigg and Aunt Magnolia wary of me, suddenly it was me and Aunt Pigg wary of Aunt Magnolia. Aunt Pigg began to come up to me when I got home from school and say things conspiratorially like, "She's doing it again. She's *thinking*. What is she thinking about?"

We could not tell what Aunt Magnolia was thinking about. Although she was weak, it was apparent that her strength was returning. Her bruises were disappearing. Her gums had stopped bleeding. But she had a frightening glint in her eye, as if some angry thought was energizing her and feeding her return to life.

"What have I done with my life, Pigg?" she would ask over dinner. She still insisted on being served on the couch although we were quite aware that she could at least hobble to the dinner table now. Aunt Pigg and I ate across the room from her at the dining room table.

"Uh . . . uh . . ." Aunt Pigg would say nervously because if you didn't say the right thing to Aunt Magnolia she would snap. Aunt Pigg said this kind of crankiness was just part of a convalescent's progress and we should ignore it, but I had my doubts. It seemed to me more as if when she began bleeding she also released the bile from the dark and twisted recesses of her soul.

"NOTHING!" barked Aunt Magnolia. "NOTHING!"

"Oh, please stop," said Aunt Pigg. We had just gotten all the trash off our lawn and become respectable again in the eyes of the neighborhood. She did not want someone thinking there were domestic disturbances going on.

"Have I gone to Spain? NO! Have I worn stiletto heels and hung out in nightclubs? NO! Have I eaten goat cheese? NO!"

"Would you like me to get you some goat cheese, Mag?" asked Aunt Pigg tremulously.

"NO!" said Aunt Magnolia. "I'm just listing my life's shortfallings. Have I swum the Great Salt Lake? NO!"

"Neither has my mother," I said, chewing ruminatively. There is nothing like someone's loud theatrics to make me cool as a cucumber. "It seems to me if someone should have swum the Great Salt Lake, it would be my mother because she wants to become a Mormon."

"Have I been trained in the ancient art of kung gu? NO!"

"I believe that is kung fu, dear," said Aunt Pigg.

"I have done NOTHING!" said Aunt Magnolia. "AB-SOLUTELY NOTHING."

"Now, I wouldn't say nothing, ex-ex-ex-exactly," said Aunt Pigg.

"I WANT TO GO TO THE BEACH!" yelled Aunt Magnolia. And then she sat up and finished her dinner quite politely as if nothing had happened. Maybe she just had to get it out of her system.

But no. It was not out of her system the next day, so to the beach we were going. All three of us, for an unspecified period of time. Aunt Pigg had to write my teacher a note saying I was leaving on the weekend and would probably be gone the last bit of school and could she please organize whatever work I needed to finish out the year so that I could do it on the road.

"Oh, of course," said my teacher when I gave her the note, "your mother disappeared in Uganda, didn't she, dear? Naturally your aunts want to take you to Africa, to be with your father. You'll be a comfort to each other." Tears welled up in her eyes. I couldn't bring myself to tell her that I was going to the beach.

On Friday my teacher and the principal sorted out the homework with me, as well as giving me a Critz Elementary T-shirt to wear in Africa.

"Don't worry about a thing," they said. I know it's one of those things that people say and they meant it kindly, but surely they can't imagine that someone whose mother has been lost in Uganda is ever going to be able to put it out of his mind for long.

The odd thing was that once we hit the road, for a while I did. For one thing, there was the giant ball of string.

Aunt Magnolia and Aunt Pigg argued in the car all the way to the giant ball of string. They argued about whether it was just another giant ball of string or the world's biggest ball of string. They argued about whether when Aunt Magnolia's doctor said, "Please leave," she meant her office or that Aunt Magnolia was well enough to travel. They argued about whether they should stop at their house in Floyd and get their swimsuits and cruise wear for warmer weather or whether to go on and buy stuff on the road as needed. But Aunt Magnolia wanted her cell phone, so they returned to Floyd and stopped at their office, where half a dozen assistants waited on them anxiously. They told the office staff to give my parents the cell phone number when they would inevitably call, having tried and failed to reach us in Critz. Then we went to their house, but I did not get to see the amazingly small backyard because they, rudely, did not invite me in but left me in the car while they packed. Then we were back on the road and I returned to sprawling in the backseat.

Aunt Magnolia should really have been sprawled in the backseat because she wasn't well enough to sit up all day yet, although, thank goodness for small favors, she was past the point where she was going to ooze blood all over the car. That would have made the trip impossible. But she seemed to think seat position denoted rank, and she refused to be relegated to backseat status. Instead, she lowered the front seat until her head was almost resting on whatever part of me happened to be lounging behind her seat. In case of an accident we would probably end up wound together like one huge sticky lump of dough. It did not bear thinking about.

After they came out of their house and threw their suitcases, presumably packed with cruise wear, into the trunk, they spent the rest of the drive arguing about whether all their cruise wear was suitable for a Virginia beach. I would like to go on record as saying that by the end of the day I hated them both all over again with a renewed passion that might have been invigorating but was a little disturbing at times. You don't like to find yourself pausing in your day to plan the best way to tie your relatives (no matter how unlovely) to railroad tracks.

By the time we finally reached the giant ball of twine (it was not string, as Aunt Pigg had said it would be; this started another argument), we were all hot and thirsty and less interested than we might otherwise have been. I wanted to go into the museum and gift shop devoted to Colonel Beaumont Wilke's twine obsession. For one thing, I was desperate for some time out of the car. But Aunt Pigg and Aunt Magnolia, having found a Coke machine outside the museum, decided this was excitement enough and refused to take me inside because of the small admission charge and their sudden passion for thrift.

"After all, if we are to stay at the beach for a month or two or three, until your parents return, then we must save our pennies," said Aunt Magnolia as we shared the one Diet Coke she had bought.

Aunt Pigg chose that unfortunate moment to put a dime into the Coke machine, preparatory to putting fourteen more in, and Aunt Magnolia slapped her hand. I think she had meant to just sort of flick it away, because when it made more solid contact than that, she looked as surprised as Aunt Pigg and me.

"OW!" said Aunt Pigg, as much in amazement as anything else.

"No more Coke for you, Pigg," said Aunt Magnolia, not wasting anyone's time by apologizing. "It's a long haul to the motel."

"Ow!" said Aunt Pigg again, making her way back to the car.

I carefully found the coin return slot, retrieved the dime, and pocketed it. As yet I had no plan to effect my egress, but one never knew.

"In fact," said Aunt Magnolia, suddenly turning around on her heel and marching back to the Coke machine, "let's get back that dime." When it wasn't there after she pushed the coin return button, she pushed it several more times increasingly harder. Then she hit the machine and kicked it. A man finally came out of the museum and said, "Here, stop that."

"This machine ate my dime," said Aunt Magnolia.

"Machine clearly states Cokes cost a buck fifty," said the man. "You can't get a Coke for a dime no more, lady."

"Yes, I know that, you nincompoop," said Aunt Magnolia. "I put a dime in and I changed my mind."

"How do I know that?" said the man. "How do I know you're not out there just trying to cadge dimes off museum owners? You wouldn't believe what we see in the tourist trade."

"I want my dime," said Aunt Magnolia.

The man just turned around and went back into the

museum. I felt like applauding. If he had given the dime to Aunt Magnolia, I would, of course, have had to come clean and return *my* dime to him. So I was doubly happy that he had not.

"Waste, Pigg. Waste, waste, waste," said Aunt Magnolia, getting back into the car. She put a beach towel over her head and said, "Drive."

It was a lovely first day on the road.

Virginia Beach

AT SUNSET we reached Virginia Beach. We were even more hot and tired and cranky. Aunt Pigg was angry because they had decided to take my parents' car, not their own, and it didn't have air-conditioning.

"I told you we should have taken our own car," said Aunt Pigg. "This means we're going to sit around and swelter and stick to seats for three months. All because you thought it was fair."

"Fair and decent. You don't ask someone to babysit your child and expect them to put wear and tear on their own car doing so."

Fortunately, they were interrupted by Aunt Magnolia's cell phone. While Aunt Pigg drove from unlikely-looking motel to unlikely-looking motel, pulling into their parking lots, doing a full circuit, and returning to the road

—apparently her motel vetting system—I talked to my father, who sounded, I must say, rather low.

"How are you, boy?" he asked gloomily.

"I'm fine," I said. I did not think I should tell him I was going to the beach. "Has anyone found Mom?"

"Your mother has been seen, and that is all I can tell you at the moment," he said. Then there was a long silence while we both tried to think of something to say.

"Was she seen from far away?" I asked in some desperation.

"I believe the gentleman who saw her was using binoculars at the time."

"Ah," I said.

"So of course we cannot be absolutely sure."

"Of course not."

"But she was wearing the orange safari shirt she left in. And another bright-colored shirt such as the student primatologist wore was seen close to her. I believe that is a positive sign and also an indication, if I may be so bold, that it was not a monkey this gentleman saw. It's quite easy from a great distance to confuse monkeys and humans."

"Really?" I said politely. "I wouldn't have thought."

It was such a relief to have a polite conversation with someone for a change.

"Where are you?" asked my father. "I called home first, of course, and when no one answered, I called the office and got Mag's cell."

"We are having dinner out," I said. Aunt Magnolia waved frantically for the phone, so I handed it reluctantly over.

"Norman?" she barked into the phone "Norman, where are you? Are you still in Africa?"

I don't know where she thought he would be, with my mother still lost.

"Yes, Norman, of course we are going to have dinner, that is, if we can ever find a motel room first. Pigg is just now pulling into the parking lot of something called the Dogs O'Doodle Motel. I can't say it looks very promising, but apparently Pigg sees something in it I don't because she is getting out of the car and walking over to the office. Oh well, it's all the same to me. Now, where are you staying tonight? A tourist rest house, you say? I must say that doesn't sound very comfortable, Norman, but at least you don't have to stay in a grass hut with a lot of anthropologists or something. *Why* are we staying in the Dogs O'Doodle? Oh yes, because Pigg and I have gone on a little vacation and taken Henry with us. Well, we couldn't leave him behind, Norman. Yes, I was having quite the time of it with my health. You might not have been kept apprised of my health issues, Norman. But now that I have discovered that I'm going to live after all, I have decided to do just that. What? Live, Norman, that's what I've been trying to tell you. And you can't live in Critz, I'm very sorry. It's just too boring. It's exactly like Floyd. No, we're going to the beach. Do Henry a world of good. He has absolutely no color. None at all. He looks like"—and here she looked at me and tactfully covered her mouth with her hand and whispered, but I heard anyway—"sow-belly." Then she handed the phone back to me.

"Son," said my father.

"Yes?" I said, so sorry that now he had yet another worry. I had been all prepared to lie about our little trip.

"Eat your apricots."

"What?" I had heard him perfectly well, but this was not at all what I had expected him to say, as you can well imagine.

"They're full of vitamins."

"I just bet they are," I said resignedly. Would no one say anything sensible, ever? Although to some, I suppose, "Eat your apricots" was as sensible as anything else.

"But try to find the ones preserved without sulfites. Sulfites are the Devil's work."

Now he was beginning to sound like a missionary.

"Will you call me if you get any more word of Mom?" I asked.

"I will, but we must do what we can in the meantime, which is what made me think of apricots. There is a short supply of reading material where I am right now. In the jungle, mostly. Staying at rather out-of-the-way places, as you can imagine."

I looked around the parking lot of the Dogs O'Doodle and could only nod.

"But someone has considerately left a pile of old *Health* magazines on a table here, so I have been brushing up," said my father in his thoughtful tone. "There was a very interesting article about apricots. Very interesting. I wish I could remember the content. But I remember the gist. Eat more of them."

My father and I share an unfortunate inability to remember the specifics of anything we read or hear. We can watch a whole fascinating *National Geographic* show about how bananas are becoming extinct, for example, and be completely riveted and then when my mother gets home from her work at the homeless shelter, and we want to share our viewing pleasure, be completely unable to tell her anything about it except that we enjoyed it immensely and learned a lot and, by the way, looks like bananas are toes up. It doesn't drive my mother crazy: she is quite accepting of others' infirmities, which is probably why she is so good with the homeless.

"Eat more of them," I said, nodding. "Well, I will."

"I miss you, boy," said my father.

"I miss you, too," I said, getting a bit lumpy in the throat area.

"I'm sure your mother misses you, too," he said. "Wherever she is."

"Wherever she is," I repeated, and then we hung up because what more was there to say?

The Dogs O'Doodle

IT WAS at that hanging-up moment that Aunt Pigg came trotting back to the car. Her perpetually upturned lips were now pursed in a definite moue.

"Mag, you may as well come in, the man at the desk says he wants one hundred and ten dollars a night for a room."

"Who does he think he is? Conrad Hilton?" asked Aunt Magnolia, dragging herself into a more upright sitting position. "Now you just go back there, Pigg, and tell him that any motel that decorates in pale turquoise and pink should know better than to demand such sums. Good golly!"

It turned out that Aunt Pigg and Aunt Magnolia hadn't once been on vacation, not even a small local one, for twenty years. Instead they had slaved to put together their design business and even now wouldn't be spending their savings on a vacation if Aunt Magnolia's body hadn't begun to destroy itself on her fortieth birthday, forcing her to think about what little time she had remaining. At least, this is what they were arguing about in front of the desk clerk, because Aunt Pigg wanted to go home now that she saw what motels cost and Aunt Magnolia wanted to push on.

"To where? They're all going to cost the same," said Aunt Pigg, who was playing with a toothpick from the container in front of the desk clerk.

"I don't know," said Aunt Magnolia, picking up a toothpick of her own and poking Aunt Pigg with it. They poked each other back and forth under the counter as they asked the clerk about the room amenities. The desk clerk looked both alarmed and bored. I bet he had looked habitually bored since starting work at the Dogs O'Doodle. The whole motel had that kind of heavy dullness.

An older couple entered. They were nicely dressed all in pastels and looked frankly shocked at my aunts' behavior before they could put on politely oblivious masks. Aunt Pigg and Aunt Magnolia immediately stopped poking. They didn't mind being playful in front of motel clerks, but they were embarrassed to be seen doing it in front of civilized traveling southerners.

"As we were saying," said Aunt Pigg in her most refined southern tones, "we'd like a room. We just had no idea prices had risen so in twenty years."

"And we will need an extra cot as well," said Aunt Magnolia. "I suppose there will be an additional charge for that." She sort of batted her eyes in the direction of the old couple in the same way that you are supposed to lie down and bare your neck to predatory wolves.

"Twenty dollars," said the clerk, going back to looking completely bored again, with some reluctance. I think he had enjoyed the excitement of his brief stab of alarm.

"Well, all right, but I don't know how motel owners can sleep at night," said Aunt Pigg.

"Sssh," said Aunt Magnolia. "Let us finish our business and allow these good folks in pink to step up to the plate."

The couple behind us hardly blinked. They smiled down at me the way you are supposed to smile down upon innocent children. I suppose they felt sorry for me. I smiled back at them and for a moment wanted to beg them to adopt me, picking up on their viewpoint and suddenly seeing myself as they saw me: a pathetic child in a bad environment with no hope for a better life. The two of them looked like nothing outrageous was ever said in their household, dinnertime was always a quiet meat-and-three affair, and measured tones were used by all.

"Come on, Henry," said Aunt Pigg and dragged me out the door. "That old lady looked like she was about to *eat* you."

"She did not," I said. "She looked perfectly respectable."

"I'm hungry," said Aunt Magnolia.

We dropped our bags in the room and went out to find a restaurant. There was a small restaurant attached to the Dogs O'Doodle office, but Aunt Magnolia and Aunt Pigg were embarrassed about the toothpicks, so we decided to dine closer to the beach. The diner we found was full of white-haired people. Everyone on the road, everyone in the motel, everyone in restaurants seemed to be white-haired. Perhaps in May with school still in session and the weather heating up, old people were taking to the road and pooling in tourist areas like ants around a banana peel. Aunt Magnolia picked at her dinner.

"Everything's brown," she said disconsolately, pointing to her deep-fried seafood plate. There were brown deep-fried scallops and brown deep-fried shrimp and brown deep-fried fish and brown french fries.

"Yes, but you love fried food, Mag, and you could never eat it before," said Aunt Pigg, digging into her salad.

"Why couldn't you eat it?" I asked Aunt Magnolia.

"Fattening," said Aunt Magnolia, patting her bony hips. "I may look naturally svelte, but I have had to struggle with my weight, Henry."

It was nice to be called Henry and not "honey" or "boy" for a change. Because I couldn't hide in a closet on the road, I resigned myself to conversations with them, and if you caught Aunt Magnolia when she wasn't hungry or sleepy or bored or restless, she really wasn't so bad.

"But now that you've lost all that weight with the flu, and that weird immune thing, you can eat whatever you like. You can have *dessert*, Mag," Aunt Pigg pointed out.

I looked at my hamburger and fries. Imagine not letting yourself have dessert. I wouldn't live that way. "I think you should have dessert anyway," I said. "I think everyone should have dessert."

"You are not a woman," said Aunt Pigg observantly.

"My mother is a woman and she always eats dessert," I said.

"That is because Katherine doesn't care how she looks," said Aunt Pigg.

"My mother looks fine," I said, rising to my feet as best I could, trapped by the booth.

"She's plump," said Aunt Mag. "She's always been a bit plump. No doubt you've never noticed. And of course, Katherine never cares what anyone thinks."

"She looks just fine," I said. I was going to say that she was beautiful, but my mother wasn't beautiful. She looked like a slightly overweight hound dog, and if you saw her on the street you might think to yourself in passing that that's what she was, a jowly old hound dog in a dress. I just loved the look of her. There wasn't another mom like her anywhere. "And," I added for stinging good measure, "she has fun."

Aunt Magnolia looked stricken for a moment and we finished our meal in silence.

After dinner Aunt Magnolia said she was too tired for a walk on the beach.

"But we've been driving all day to get here!" said Aunt Pigg. "Don't you even want to swing by and perhaps have a crawl on the beach?"

"There's no need to be sarcastic," said Aunt Magnolia. "Neither one of you has had a life-threatening illness. You have no idea how tired out and drawn it makes you."

"I know you're tired out, Mag, but just to take a look," said Aunt Pigg. "Or perhaps we could drop you off at the motel and Henry and I could swing back to take a walk on the beach."

As soon as Aunt Pigg mentioned this possibility, Aunt Magnolia pulled herself together. "Never mind. If you're so stuck on the idea, let us go to the beach."

"No, no," Aunt Pigg said. "If you're really too tired, Mag."

"No, I don't want to make you drive all the way back to the motel just to drop me off. I feel much revived by my entirely brown dinner and ready for anything."

"Not if you really feel depleted, Mag," said Aunt Pigg.

"Drive," said Aunt Magnolia.

So we drove mostly what seemed to be in circles until quite by accident we ended up at a parking lot by the beach, and there lay the Atlantic, spread out before us like a great mystery between us and a whole lot of people we didn't know on the other side. I was suddenly aware not just of all those people off in Europe looking in our direction over the waves, wondering about us, but of all the billions of things moving and alive beneath the water. All those life forms that never even knew of an existence miles above them. All of this happening every day without any thought of us, or us with any thought of it. Sometimes you can get so closed into your little corner of the world you forget all the stuff like the ocean going on without you thinking about it, while you breathe somewhere else.

The day had been hot and sticky, but the beach sand felt cool under my feet and the air felt so clear it was as if it were cleaning me. I took off my shoes and ran down to the water's edge, being careful of rogue waves because I had once heard you could be washed out to sea and never seen again. "Last one in is a rotten egg," called Aunt Pigg, and she ran right into the water with all her clothes on. I stood gaping onshore. Aunt Magnolia hobbled slowly down toward us. She really did look like death still, and I began to think Aunt Pigg and I had been too hard on her at dinner. Maybe she was doing the best she could under crabby circumstances. "Well?" she said as she reached me. "Aren't you going to leap in and ruin all your clothes, too?"

So I did.

The Beach

AUNT PIGG GOT LOST on the way back to the motel. We
didn't have a map and it was twilight by the time we left
the beach. Aunt Magnolia fell asleep in the front seat,
and so I had to help Aunt Pigg navigate.

"No, I think it's here. I'm sure we already passed that
large blinking orange," I said, pointing to a sign advertis-
ing something with oranges, I guess. Aunt Pigg must have
been tired, too, because she didn't say much but kept
driving around in circles with a kind of pathetic hopeful-
ness. Finally, when we were passing what I was sure was
the same corner for the umpteenth time, but must not
have been after all, we saw the Dogs O'Doodle and we
were so tired and so glad to see it, it was like coming
home.

We pulled quietly into the parking lot. Because all the
old people were staying there it had a hushed quality that

was very soothing. I was glad we had already unloaded our suitcases and could just tumble in and dry off. We woke up Aunt Magnolia, who didn't speak to us, not out of any unpleasantness but just out of a kind of exhaustion, I think. The motel staff had already set up my cot in a corner of the room.

"I can't sleep there," I said, looking at the two of them. I found it hard enough to sleep in the same house with them. I certainly couldn't sleep in the same room. "I'll just put some pillows in the bathtub." I started to carry pillows in there, but they wouldn't let me. They said they often needed the facilities in the middle of the night. I hated it that they called the bathroom "the facilities," and sat on my cot holding my pajamas in my arms, waiting while Aunt Magnolia got changed in the bathroom. She got to go first because she was supposedly always the most tired. I thought sleepily that this was debatable. She came out wearing a long flannel granny gown and with a contraption over her nose. "Snore stopper," whispered Aunt Pigg to me. Aunt Magnolia got into bed, lay down on her back, put a sleep mask with some kind of blue gel in it that made her look like an alien over her eyes and earplugs in her ears, and folded her hands over her chest.

Why don't we just bury her? I thought, and tromped into the bathroom. I got into bed with the flashlight I had packed and tried the best I could to make a privacy tent of my covers. This was about as hateful a situation as a boy could find himself in. I didn't even have the energy to read a book. I read Archie comics and hated the universe.

Aunt Pigg went into the bathroom and came out wearing a similar granny gown. She got into bed also with a sleep mask and earplugs but without the snore stopper. She turned up the air-conditioning and turned off the light. Then, I guess, she couldn't sleep, because she got out her radio, took the earplugs out, and put headphones on. Even so, I could hear the low drone of it for what felt like hours. I could not sleep. I had no sleep mask or earplugs, and I defy you to find anything worse than the sound of your aunts' breathing all night long in the motel room dark. I felt awful. Gritty. I couldn't figure out why. Then I realized it was the salt. I should have showered it off, but I had never been swimming in the ocean before and didn't know that salt stuck to you so. I felt like one of the brown salted things sitting on someone's dinner plate. My dreams were not tranquil.

The motel had a free Continental breakfast, which meant gently sweating doughnuts, orange juice, and coffee in the lobby.

"This is not a proper breakfast," complained Aunt Magnolia, who was wearing her cruise wear and felt armed with respectability again. An older gentleman appeared behind the motel desk.

"Good morning," he said. "Help yourself. I hope you're enjoying your stay in Virginia Beach."

Aunt Magnolia looked at him as if she defied him to have the impertinence to speak again. She was not a morning person.

I guess this got the gentleman's goat because he obviously thought of himself as the beneficent host. "Allow me to introduce myself. One of my boys got sick, so I said I would come in. Owned the Dogs O'Doodle for thirty years now."

"Mr. Doodle, I presume?" said Aunt Magnolia.

"Mr. O'Doodle," said the man as if that made a world of difference.

We nodded to him politely and ate our doughnuts under his watchful eye, while I wondered if his first name was Dogs, but was too shy to ask.

"Well, Pigg, I think it's time we went to the beach," said Aunt Magnolia.

"Oh, Mag," said Aunt Pigg as we climbed into the car, "I've been waiting for this day for so many years, I cannot count. A day in the sun."

"Yes," said Aunt Magnolia dreamily. "No clients, no phone calls, nothing to do but read and soak up rays."

I must admit the beach was hot. I do not know why I didn't expect this. I guess when you see beaches in magazine ads they look as if they are always a temperature for perfect comfort. We put our towels down, and Aunt Mag and Aunt Pigg lay on the sand where flies would land on them and then apparently change their minds. I watched this for a while. Then Aunt Magnolia sat up. "I'm too hot, Pigg," she said.

"I know what you mean," said Aunt Pigg. "But let's give it a while longer."

They lay down again, and then Aunt Magnolia said, "How much longer?"

"Maybe we should get wet first," said Aunt Pigg. "Then we'll be just the right temperature."

"I don't want to get in the water," said Aunt Magnolia. So Aunt Pigg went down to the water alone. She came back screaming. There were long thin whip marks over one shin.

"Jellyfish," said Aunt Magnolia reflectively. "I've seen them on the Discovery Channel. Must be very painful."

"Argh, argh, argh!" Aunt Pigg was shouting and hopping around on the good leg.

"Well, just lie down and put some wet sand on it," suggested Aunt Magnolia.

"Is that what you're supposed to do?" asked Aunt Pigg.

"I don't know," said Aunt Magnolia, lying back down herself and closing her eyes. "You know, I think I'm beginning to enjoy this. I feel a cool breeze stirring."

It was more like a wind, and as it picked up, it blew hot sand in our eyes. I could feel sand in my teeth and hair. The wind became so strong and the surf so loud that within an hour we could hardly hear each other speak. Which wasn't necessarily a bad thing.

When the wind finally died down again, it was midafternoon and I was ravenous. We had been having unsatisfying meals of chips and chocolate bars and Cokes from a kiosk on the beach. That is, Aunt Magnolia and I had. Aunt Pigg had been eating something called Thinners, which were some kind of make-believe potato chips made out of wood fiber and covered in seasoned salt. They looked terrible. I asked Aunt Pigg if they were healthy. She thought about it and said that they were low in calories, so they were at least neutral. A lot of food Aunt Pigg ate seemed to be neutral.

"I never thought I would find myself eating wood," said Aunt Pigg as she finished the dregs in the bag.

"I wouldn't mind staying so very thin if I didn't feel so half here," said Aunt Magnolia. "As if I were transparent."

"You're not *that* thin, I hate to tell you, Mag," said Aunt Pigg.

"Is that all there is, then?" asked Aunt Magnolia.

"Is that all there is to what?" asked Aunt Pigg.

"To a vacation on the beach."

"Is *what* all there is?" asked Aunt Pigg.

"Lying here eating forbidden junk food which, and I'm sure you agree with me, Henry," said Aunt Magnolia, "just makes you feel awful, not happy and larkish at all, after a while."

"It's made *me* bilious," I said.

"Bilious?" said Aunt Magnolia. "What kind of word is that for a ten-year-old to use?"

"I'm twelve," I said. Aunt Magnolia was always forgetting my particulars.

"He probably read it in a book. Henry is a bookish young man," said Aunt Pigg, who spent a lot of time, it seemed to me, softening Aunt Magnolia up so she wouldn't explode in our faces.

I had actually read it in a book just that morning and the meaning was obvious. I had read most of my book on the beach. I didn't want to go into the water. I wasn't afraid of jellyfish or rogue waves, I just hadn't had much sleep what with the snore stopper that didn't work and the rattling breaths of my emaciated decaying aunts. I longed for a normal-sized woman like my mother who wasn't so concerned about dieting and doing her nails and stuff. But I supposed it had something to do with Aunt Magnolia and Aunt Pigg being single.

" 'Bilious' is a perfectly good word," I said.

"It's a perfectly good word, but it makes you sound peculiar to use antiquated language like that," said Aunt Magnolia, getting up and shaking sand out of her towel. Aunt Pigg and I did the same. It seemed as if we were once more on the move. Aunt Pigg and I trudged behind Aunt Magnolia, who was heading back to the car.

Aunt Pigg made us wait by the cement barrier around

the parking lot while she sat on it and brushed off sand from between her toes and put her sandals back on.

"Anyhow, you didn't answer my question," said Aunt Magnolia. "Is this all there is to a vacation on the beach?"

"Yes, I believe it is," said Aunt Pigg.

The next day we headed for the mountains.

Shenandoah

WE DROVE FOR TWO DAYS until Aunt Magnolia found something she wanted to see. I found this disconcerting.

"I thought we were spending three months at the beach," I said, because in my head that was how I had seen it. Me doing my schoolwork in the morning and then going to the beach in the afternoon or vice versa. I knew I could do all my schoolwork for each day in about two hours. A lot of school time is just sitting around and listening or talking or drawing or stuff. If you take out all the filler parts, the actual school time is only about two hours a day. But now here I was in the backseat of our car doing my work as we drove along, and that was very distracting because the scenery was pretty spectacular. My parents weren't ones for car trips anywhere. My father actually didn't want to go anywhere at all because he was on the road so much. Busman's holiday it would be, said my mother, so we didn't. When we needed a vacation we rented a cabin on Cushinaw Lake, and that was fine. This destinationless trip made me feel more as if I were being kidnapped.

"Not anymore," said Aunt Magnolia in answer to my question. "Now we're just on vacation."

"But where are we going?" I asked.

"Anywhere we like. That's what a vacation is," said Aunt Pigg.

I thought about this. At first I accepted it and then I remembered all the vacations that the kids I knew took. They sounded pretty planned to me. You didn't just drive around looking for stuff for three months. When I mentioned this, Aunt Pigg said, "But that's what we're doing. We're driving around looking for stuff. Well put, Henry."

Then Aunt Magnolia, who was studying a map, said, "Oh, let's go check out Shenandoah," and I got excited about the trip again.

"Now, that's something I'd like to see!" I said enthusiastically because my mother used to sing me a song called "Shenandoah" when she rocked me to sleep as a baby. I didn't remember *that*, of course, but sometimes she sang it to me still when I was sick. Or couldn't sleep. Naturally, I wasn't going to tell my aunts, but it sounded like a beautiful place—"away, you rolling river"—and I wanted to see it, too. So I settled down in the backseat and didn't whine anymore about our changed plans.

The day got increasingly warm as we drove and drove and drove. We pulled into a drive-through for lunch. I got a hamburger and fries and a milk shake. Aunt Magnolia got a hamburger, fries, and a milk shake. Aunt Pigg got a large tossed green salad with diet dressing. Aunt Magnolia didn't want to sit in the hot parking lot eating and didn't want to go into the restaurant with its "grubby locals." She told Aunt Pigg that the only way to stay cool was to get onto the highway and drive with the windows open. This may be what rankled and started the argument because Aunt Pigg gave in. She kept giving in to Aunt Magnolia because Aunt Magnolia had almost died. Or might have, had she had something more serious than she turned out to have had. Anyhow, so we were driving down the highway and Aunt Pigg was trying to drive and maneuver that little plastic fork into the greens, which were dripping with the salad dressing that Aunt Magnolia had tried to pour on the salad. And Aunt Pigg said, "You know, you missed the salad. Half the salad dressing is dripping off the side of the plastic salad container."

"Well, I'm sorry," said Aunt Magnolia, "but I hate these little foil containers of dressing. They never tear at the tear-here part, and when you use enough force to rip them apart, the dressing goes everywhere, and it's hard to do when you're in a moving car."

Aunt Pigg just grunted. She kept trying to carefully ease greens up to her mouth while driving with the other hand, the thumb of which was also holding on to the plastic salad container by pressing it against the steering wheel. About 50 percent of the time, at the last second her forkful of greens would land in her lap. It must have been very frustrating and the car would slow down to about thirty-five miles an hour whenever she attempted a forkful. Finally the car behind us sped up and passed, its driver giving us the finger.

"Avert your eyes, honey," said Aunt Pigg to me.

Aunt Magnolia and I were slurping on our milk shakes, and you could see Aunt Pigg's gaze wandering over in our direction every time we slurped and the great self-control she was mustering to keep from poking our eyes out. I think part of her problem was that she was always hungry to more or less of a degree. It was true, she was as slim as a girl, but it seemed to me she paid a terrible price.

"Would you like a fry?" I asked her.

"No, thank you, honey," said Aunt Pigg. When I tried to pass them to her anyway, thinking maybe a fry or two would improve her mood, she snapped, "Get those things out of my face."

"No need to snap at the boy, Pigg," said Aunt Magnolia. "You know, I think we should try to find someplace with a pool for tonight. Now, I know it will cost a little bit extra—"

"I'm not the one banging dimes out of Coke machines," said Aunt Pigg.

"I didn't say you were," said Aunt Magnolia, sounding mortally offended. She had obviously been feeling cheery and magnanimous. But she had had waffles for breakfast and a milk shake for lunch. There's a lesson in there for you, I thought.

"Henry, would you like a dip in a pool tonight?" Aunt Pigg asked me.

"I don't care," I said, trying to be polite.

"Well, the boy doesn't care, so let's just get something convenient. If it comes with a pool, fine," said Aunt Pigg, who was clearly sick of driving.

"But *I* would like a pool," said Aunt Magnolia. "You know, I think I prefer pools to the beach. I think the reason I didn't like the beach was that you got so *dirty* there. So gritty and sandy and salty. You just never felt clean. But I could see myself slipping into a pool and swimming back and forth, back and forth, all evening."

"Well, if you've got so much energy, Mag, why don't *you* drive for a change," said Aunt Pigg, and you could tell she was getting really mad because the car started to go faster and faster.

"You're doing a very good job at the wheel, Pigg," said Aunt Magnolia serenely.

"What do you mean, 'doing a good job'?" said Aunt

Pigg. "I'm exhausted. I've been driving since nine o'clock this morning and we won't be near where you've *decided you want to go*"—she said this in a particularly nasty tone of voice—"until suppertime. It's not a threat, it's a perfectly reasonable question: if you're feeling well enough to swim, why don't you take a turn driving?"

I slumped down in the backseat and asked to borrow Aunt Pigg's radio. I put on her earphones and tuned Aunt Pigg and Aunt Magnolia out. It wasn't easy because by this time they were *loud.* I couldn't hear the particulars, but you could tell from the rhythm of the car speeding up and slowing down and an occasional shouted word that everything either one of them had done to the other since childhood was being rehashed. I tried to concentrate on my schoolwork and the music, but I couldn't find any music I liked, so I kept turning the dial until I found a call-in show with a psychologist. I liked her voice, and the things she told people seemed to be helpful and interesting, so I stayed there, looking at the Blue Ridge Mountains and listening to the soothing sound of her voice. I wished I could have put a beach towel over my head, but when I tried, the wind from the open window kept blowing it around and I could hear Aunt Pigg snap something at me, too, so I took it off and slumped lower in my seat, and by the time we got to the motel Aunt Pigg and Aunt Magnolia weren't speaking to each other anymore, so at least it was quiet.

We pulled into the parking lot of a pink motel around four o'clock. Aunt Pigg found one with a pool because she could never be spiteful about little things like that. We were off the road earlier than Aunt Pigg had thought we would be, and that seemed to put her in a better frame of mind.

"Yep," she said, "I made good time."

"Last one in is a rotten egg," said Aunt Magnolia, who changed into her swimsuit and headed for the pool. Aunt Pigg turned up the air-conditioning and did all the little housekeepery things she liked to do in a motel room. She moved the Kleenex box to her night table and took all the waxed paper off the drinking glasses and unwrapped the soaps in the bathroom. Then she went to the Coke machine and got a bucket of ice and a nice cold Coke and sat in the little chair outside the door, stretching her feet and drinking from a heavily sweating glass. It must have felt like heaven after all that driving. I don't think Aunt Pigg was a natural driver. She drove with a studied frown on her face the whole way, whether, as today, we were going slowly up the mountains or whether we were on the downward slope to the sea.

Aunt Magnolia was splashing away in the pool, having a wonderful time.

"Don't you want a swim?" asked Aunt Pigg. I suspect she wanted to get rid of me. Finding time alone on this trip was going to be a problem.

I looked at her Coke glass. Reluctantly she followed my eyes and said, "I'm sorry, honey, I didn't even ask you if you wanted a Coke, too. It sure is a hot day. Now you go in and get my purse off of the desk in there and I'll see if I can find you some change." So she did, and I took my Coke tactfully out to poolside. I didn't really want to get into the pool with Aunt Magnolia, who was splashing around with such abandon that she was frankly rather alarming me. In the end I took a cool shower, and then when Aunt Magnolia came in to fling herself on a bed, I ran out and jumped in for a quick swim. The ladies (as I also came to think of them in my head when they weren't behaving too terribly) were hungry and wanted an early dinner. As I swam I saw a boy delivering the cot to our room. We had a little routine going now, I thought happily. I didn't know how much I liked routine before starting this open-ended vacation. I liked routine, but I also liked knowing that I didn't know what would happen next and would just have to handle it the best I could. So far I thought I was doing pretty well.

We were all cooled off again and feeling hopeful about dinner as we drove into town. Aunt Magnolia and Aunt Pigg both said they didn't care where we ate, so I suggested this restaurant that looked kind of nice. Aunt Magnolia said fine, as long as it didn't have a nautical theme. I guess Captain Sam's had scarred her. But then we had to sit for a long time waiting for the menus and Aunt Pigg had only eaten that salad for lunch and Aunt Magnolia was impatient by nature, and dinner was terrible. I had a hamburger and fries and a milk shake. The milk shake didn't seem to have any ice cream in it, and the fries looked like dead slugs. The hamburger had a piece of lettuce in it that was more brown than green. I looked at my dinner plate with dismay but didn't say anything, especially as Aunt Pigg and Aunt Magnolia were looking at their dinners the same way. No one said anything until we left, when Aunt Magnolia said, "That's the last time *you* pick the restaurant." It was so venomous it took me by surprise, and then I had to turn my head away because my eyes were stinging. It had been a long time since I'd seen my mother, and she would never have said anything like that to me. She would have joked about it or something. *Something* light and easy. My mother never said anything to hurt anyone. At least not on purpose.

"I guess that's it for the night; let's go on home," said Aunt Pigg disconsolately. We were all feeling the strain of the day, and a kind of trip weariness had set in.

"Oh no, Pigg, I can't sit around that hotel room all night. It's only six-thirty, for heaven's sakes," said Aunt Magnolia.

"Well, what do you want to do?" asked Aunt Pigg in even tones.

"I don't know," said Aunt Magnolia, "but there must be something to do around here."

We were standing in the air-conditioned vestibule by the door, not ready to tackle the humidity yet, and a white-haired gentleman who was coming in, leaning on a cane, said, "Hey, pardon my interruption, ladies, but if you're looking for something to do, the entrance to the Appalachian Trail is only a few miles up the road."

"The Appalachian Trail. Now, there's an idea. I've always wanted to see that, Pigg," said Aunt Magnolia. "Let's get a map and head over there."

"Brochures at tourist information just around the corner. You can walk from here," said the man, tipping his hat. "You pack yourself a nice picnic lunch and head on out there tomorrow at sunrise. Wonderful views up there. Simply wonderful. Wonderful way to spend the day. The missus and I used to do it back when I could still walk. And she was still alive," he added as an afterthought.

We thanked him and he nodded his head. I think I'd like to be an old southern gentleman like that when I grow up. My mother is always telling me not to do this or that or I'll get Yankee manners, so I'm always glad I was lucky enough to be born in the South. I know you're not supposed to want to be just a southern gentlemen these days. Although, of course, you could be a southern gentleman and just about anything else, too. But if you told people you wanted to be a southern gentleman they would think you were soft. People despise you if they think you're too soft.

We started to walk toward the tourist info place and Aunt Pigg said, "What a nice old gentleman. Let's find a grocery store tomorrow and get picnic food and do what he says: take a nice long hike and have a picnic. We can have an early evening tonight."

"But Pigg, I'm all perky," said Aunt Magnolia. "I want to go now."

"Hike *now*, Mag?" said Aunt Pigg.

"I don't mean hike, I mean just drive up the road to the entrance and maybe just have a little walk in to take a look."

"I'm so tired, Mag. Honestly. Oh, Mag . . . Well . . ." said Aunt Pigg.

So we got the maps and Aunt Pigg drove us farther up the mountain until we found the path that led to the Appalachian Trail. The brochure said that it went 2,160 miles all the way from Georgia to Maine and some people hiked the whole distance. We got out at the parking lot, and there were all kinds of bear warnings and stuff.

"Isn't it awfully late to be heading into the woods?" asked Aunt Pigg again.

"You mean, during bear suppertime," asked Aunt Magnolia and laughed evilly.

"I mean, with darkness falling," said Aunt Pigg, but it was still quite light out, so Aunt Magnolia just looked at her until Aunt Pigg sighed and we headed down the path to the trail. We were the only car in the parking lot and we saw no one on the path. The silence was profound.

We had to hike quite a long way in, and Aunt Magnolia, for some reason, was wearing her flip-flops, so I could see a slow burn beginning again between the two aunts, who were trying to figure out new ways to blame each other. It probably would have been nice in the morning, in those woods, but tired, at the end of a long day, with nothing all around us but the sameness of the dense walls of the forest and endless plodding, we were beginning to feel irritable again. How Aunt Pigg could blame Aunt Magnolia for this was fairly obvious; I was curious to see how Aunt Magnolia was going to blame Aunt Pigg. But then the path opened onto the Appalachian Trail itself and there was the Shenandoah Valley spread out before us like a dream. A soft twilight was descending and there were clouds hanging over the valley, the blue haze of the mountains was poured upon the earth, and the sky was a collage of color as the sun set. And one lone star shone first, like a beacon for the others to come. Aunt Pigg and Aunt Magnolia and I sat on a rock and looked quietly down over it all.

"Daniel Boone probably came through here," said Aunt Pigg.

"Yep," said Aunt Magnolia.

"You know, he would settle someplace but as soon as he saw the smoke from someone else's chimney, meaning there were humans settling in sight of his homestead, he would move on."

"Now, that's a loner," agreed Aunt Magnolia.

"I don't know," said Aunt Pigg. "Maybe he never felt alone. I bet these mountains are good enough company. I bet maybe people kind of made him feel crowded. I bet being in these mountains was, well, I can't put it right, like the perfect relationship for him. Like a marriage."

I think this startled us so much that Aunt Magnolia and I just looked at Aunt Pigg for a second. But you couldn't keep your eyes off that Shenandoah Valley for long. We sat at cliff edge, dangling our feet over, just in that startling moment, happy as we'd ever been.

The Mall

WE SPENT the whole next day driving. Aunt Magnolia couldn't find any stuff on the map to check out and Aunt Pigg was busy keeping her eyes on the road. At first we were driving north, and then Aunt Magnolia decided she wanted to see some blue grass in Kentucky, so Aunt Pigg made her way silently south. She had hoped that Aunt Magnolia would be helping with the driving now that she was feeling better, but Aunt Magnolia hurt her accelerator foot coming off the Appalachian Trail. We had stayed so long on the cliff edge that it was beginning to get dark by the time we made our way off the trail and onto the path to the parking lot, and then it got very dark in a big hurry. Lots faster than it did at home. Aunt Magnolia said it was because the sun dropped over the mountains and darkness fell kerplop at that point. She said it was that way when they lived with my mother in Tennessee, on their father's farm up in the foothills of the Appalachians. It was twilight, twilight, twilight, then kerplop, night. She was in the middle of telling us this as we made our slightly panicked way down the path in complete darkness when she suddenly screamed. Aunt Pigg grabbed for me, thinking that Aunt Magnolia had seen a bear. Perhaps was even being chawed on by one. It sounded that way. But what had happened was that something had snagged Aunt Magnolia's right flip-flop and torn it right off her foot. She was pretty sure it was a stick of some kind, but in case it was indeed the teeth of some low-lying animal, she didn't want to stop and find out.

"Hurry, run! Run!" she called to us as we galloped down the path ahead of her in, retrospectively, a rather cowardly self-centered way. I mean we didn't even turn around to see if she was *okay*. And it wasn't until we got to the car that we discovered Aunt Magnolia had run back with only one flip-flop on, and the bottom of her right flip-flopless foot had a big hole where she had stepped on something, "or been *bitten*," she reminded us.

Aunt Pigg was so relieved that Aunt Magnolia was okay that she snapped, "Serves you right for wearing *flip-flops* into the woods. You're lucky something worse didn't happen to you!"

"What worse could there be?" asked Aunt Magnolia as she held her bloody foot in her lap while Aunt Pigg drove us back to the motel room.

"It could have been *both* feet," said Aunt Pigg after a pause to consider. She fairly spat it out. She was really annoyed with Aunt Magnolia, partly for putting herself in danger, I think, but also, I suspect, because she had thought she was finally going to get some help with the driving and now she could see that hope turning to dust.

When we got back to the motel and Aunt Magnolia had washed off her foot with many cries of anguish and all the motel room towels and washcloths, leaving Aunt Pigg and me with nothing to dry ourselves with after showers except our still-sandy beach towels or bloody bath towels, it turned out that Aunt Magnolia's foot, while painful, didn't look as if it required stitches or medical attention. Aunt Pigg wanted to take her into emergency anyway to get a tetanus shot, but that was just spite.

And so our next day in the car was quiet. Aunt Magnolia had bought herself a fashion magazine and had on sunglasses, to block us out, I think, and was turning the pages and loudly sucking on lemon drops. Aunt Pigg drove with a lot of tension in her neck. You could tell she was going to be in need of a massage by the end of the day. I thought about telling her about this kind of heating pad my mother uses on her neck that you put in the microwave, but then I remembered we were staying in motels without microwaves and I took another look at her back and decided not to say anything.

By lunchtime Aunt Pigg was really feeling like she

needed to make a stand, I think. I have no older brothers or sisters, so I haven't experienced the kind of grinding-into-the-dust power they apparently assert, but my friends have told me what it's like, and I must say, I could sometimes see it with Aunt Pigg, who was the younger. Every so often, my friends said, you must take a stand, even if it ends up being like Custer's and ends in slaughter all over the Plains. This was apparently Aunt Pigg's, and if it was over something seemingly trivial like lunch, so be it.

"I'm not going to try to eat a salad and drive again," she said. It was addressed to the general audience in the car, but I knew she meant it for Aunt Magnolia.

"All right," said Aunt Magnolia who kept turning pages with a desultory air. "So order a hamburger."

"No, thank you, I don't care to put on weight in all the wrong places." Aunt Pigg took her eyes off the road for a moment and rested them on Aunt Magnolia's hips, which, while not meaty, were certainly more flowing than the rest of her.

Aunt Magnolia turned and said, "Keep your eyes on the road."

And that's when Aunt Pigg pulled off at an exit and headed into a large gray nondescript mall's parking lot. "Food court," she said.

Aunt Magnolia said she wasn't hungry and shuffled along behind Aunt Pigg, limping rather more than necessary.

"It's twelve o'clock, Mag," said Aunt Pigg. "We always lunch at noon."

"Perhaps the boy isn't hungry," said Aunt Magnolia. I hated it when they talked about me like I wasn't even there.

"I could eat," I said. "Aunt Pigg, do you think there's a bookstore in the mall? Because I'm down to my last chapter and I've brought along seven dollars and ten cents, so maybe I could buy a book."

"What can you buy for seven dollars?" called Aunt Magnolia from in back of us. I was walking tactfully between Aunt Pigg, who was barreling determinedly forward across the huge expanse of mall parking lot toward an entrance, and Aunt Magnolia, who was limping along with great show to no effect behind.

"For heaven's sakes, Mag, he doesn't need to spend his seven dollars. We can buy the boy some books," said Aunt Pigg. "After we eat."

"I'm sure my parents would pay you back for any books you bought me." I joined in eagerly because truthfully this had worried me; one book was not going to see me through. I was going through almost one a day as it was.

"Buy some that are thick and engrossing," said Magnolia. "And cheap."

We found the food court and split up. I got a burger and fries and a milk shake. Aunt Magnolia, despite the fact she said she wasn't hungry, got a large plate of bilious-looking red-sauced Chinese food. Aunt Pigg got a tossed green salad with diet dressing, a coffee, and a can of Diet Coke.

"We're going to have to have pit stops every ten miles, I can see," said Aunt Magnolia when we reconvened at one of those horrible school-desk-type table arrangements where everything is conveniently bolted to the floor.

"Don't be crude," said Aunt Pigg. "On top of every-thing else."

It wasn't until we were almost done eating that Aunt Magnolia said, "*What* everything else?"

"Oh, look," said Aunt Pigg, getting up to dump her trash and put her tray away, "a bookstore!" We must have been in a very literate town because there was such a long line to get to the bookstore cash register that it snaked right out of the bookstore. Everything else in the mall looked pretty dead.

"Where are we?" I asked Aunt Pigg.

"I have no idea," said Aunt Pigg. "All these big malls outside towns look the same."

"Somewhere people like to read, apparently," said Aunt Magnolia, joining us.

"There must be something more going on. Let's check it out," said Aunt Pigg, whose mood always improved af-ter her meals, slim though they were.

It was a book signing. The author was sitting at a table in the back of the store and there were actually two lineups: one to buy her book and one to have her autograph it. There were two whole tables with copies of her books. We picked one up to see who she was, and I got excited.

"Look at this! Look at this!" I said, pointing to her name on the cover. "It's the woman I heard on the radio the other day. It's Daly Kramer! What's she doing here? She's supposed to be in New York City."

"And here she is in a mall in Kentucky. It's a miracle," said Aunt Magnolia languidly but pushing past me to get a look. "Actually"—she cleared her throat—"I happen to have listened to her show once or twice myself." She was acting all nonchalant the way some people do around celebrities, but you could tell she was excited, too.

The book was called *How to Put Your Life Back in Order*, and I could see why that would be such a popular topic, although it presupposed that your life had ever been in order to begin with. "Come on," said Aunt Pigg to Aunt Magnolia, "let's buy a copy of her book and have her autograph it to us."

"Yes, let's!" said Aunt Magnolia, who was usually so penny-conscious, and they went off to get in the book-selling line and I went to look at the children's book section. I had to be careful: the youth section was right by the autographing line, and I kept getting stepped on as people craned their heads to see Daly Kramer. There was one guy who didn't even have a copy of her book, wasn't even in line, but who stood right by me, trying to catch glimpses of her without being obvious. He stepped on me quite a bit until a woman who was coming back from Daly Kramer's table with a signed book tripped over me and fell against him and we all went onto the floor. For a minute people stopped looking at Daly Kramer, which must have been a relief for her, and looked at us instead. But after a while they lost interest in us, when it was evident we didn't have any more amazing feats worked out, and went back to staring at Daly Kramer.

"Ow!" said the man the woman fell on when it seemed safe to say something without an audience taking notes.

"I'm just so, so sorry, I really am," said the woman, giving him a hand up. I had already gotten up on my own and resumed my search for thick, engrossing cheap novels. "They should really have this book signing outside the store to accommodate the crowds, shouldn't they? Have you had your book signed yet? No, I see you haven't."

"No, I'm not going to buy a book. I just came in to see what the fuss was about. I didn't even know she was here. You know, she's my favorite. She's just my hero. And today's my birthday! How about that? Finding Daly Kramer in a bookstore on my birthday!"

"Oh, then you *must* get her book," said the woman. "It's just meant to be. Get one and have her sign it 'Happy Birthday.'"

"No, it's okay," said the man. "I just wanted to get a look at her."

"But it's your birthday," protested the woman again.

"Look, I've only got eighteen bucks on me," said the man. "But maybe I'll work up the nerve to say hello."

"I don't think they'll let you up there without a book," said the woman, opening her wallet. She took out ten dollars and handed it to him before he had a chance to register what she was doing. "Here, buy the book. Happy birthday," she said, turned, and was out of the store like a shot. Both the man and I watched her with our mouths slightly open as she went down the maze of dark corridors where she disappeared finally into the bowels of the mall. Then I noticed that Aunt Magnolia, standing in line still, was looking, too. When she saw me she opened the book and pretended to be very engrossed in it. The man picked up a copy of the book from one of the tables, paid for it, and got in line to have it signed.

Pigg and Mag finally got their book signed and paid for a bagful of books for me. I had begun to think of them as Pigg and Mag, at least in my head, because "Aunt Magnolia" was just too much of a mouthful and "Aunt Pigg" sounded as if I should have a bunch of barnyard relatives hanging around: Cousin Rooster and Sister Hen, Brother Bull and Grandma Goat.

When we got back to the car I started a new book and Aunt Magnolia read out loud to Aunt Pigg for a while and the blue grass of Kentucky rolled by our doors.

Chet

WE STAYED at a nicer-than-usual place that night. It was pink stucco, like so many of the motels, but it had two stories and backed onto a horse farm, and as we had a second-story room we could sit in our metal chairs on our balcony and watch the horses run the length of the hills. It was like motel and entertainment built into one.

"It's too bad so many horses have to earn their keep," said Mag. She had her hurt foot propped up on the railing of the balcony and was sipping a long, tall Seven-Up with slurpy abandon.

"What would you have them do, Mag?" asked Pigg.

"Just run free like that. Just run back and forth and back and forth, bursting their little lungs with the effort if they've a mind to," said Mag contentedly. "Or eat some grass."

"Or hay," I said.

"No, just nice green grass. That's all horses really want to do. They just want to eat. Their instincts are to nose around in the dirt, nuzzling little bits of grass out of the ground. Or spook and run. They're prey."

"They're what?" said Pigg.

"You know, not predatory animals. Not predators. They're prey. Now, your dog—he's a predator. That's why you can be friends with a dog. Because they aren't hardwired to run from you. But a horse is. Man's alliance with the horse is not a natural thing."

"At least for the horse," said Pigg.

"How do you know so much about it?" I asked. Because sometimes Mag surprised me. She was the last person I thought would care about an animal—any animal, but especially something so big and inconvenient as a horse.

"We grew up with a couple of old horses," said Pigg in the stunned voice she and my mom and Mag used if they ever talked about their growing up. As if it were a whole other lifetime ago, so remote that it was like recalling a book they'd read once.

"Yep, Chip and Barn."

"You named your horse Barn?" I asked incredulously.

"Daddy did," said Mag. She and Pigg were sucking slowly and ruminatively at their drinks. Something was going on, I thought. Something was going on the same in both their heads that I didn't know about. "You do know where we are, don't you, Pigg?"

"Don't even say it, Mag," said Pigg.

"Right across the border, honey. Right across the border."

"What's right across the border? The border of what?" I asked, but they didn't answer until later when we were sitting at another air-conditioned family restaurant and I was eating a hamburger, milk shake, and fries and Mag was eating barbecue and Pigg was eating a small plain hamburger patty with a scoop of cottage cheese and two pineapple rings and some wilty lettuce.

"Border of what?" I persisted, and Mag finally answered because the two of us were trying to keep our minds off Pigg's dinner, which looked disgusting. "Have a fry?" I asked, but she was so disheartened she just waved it away silently.

"When I was ten and Mom died, we moved from Virginia to a farm in Kentucky that Daddy bought. Well, not a working farm, a broken-down old piece of land that was half in Kentucky and half in Tennessee, so that no matter where you were on it, you were right across the border, so that's what he named the farm. Right Across the Border. Stupid name, really. Like Barn for a horse."

"Oh Lord, Mag. Let's just skip it. How are we ever going to explain why we never invited him down to any of Katherine's holiday meals? How can we take this grown twelve-year-old boy there and say, Here's the grandson you kind of missed out on?"

"How about, because he just isn't NICE? Why would he get invited to Katherine's dinners anyhow? He stopped speaking to her when she was thirteen."

"My grandfather stopped speaking to Mom when she was thirteen?" I asked.

"He couldn't handle her. She was always breaking all his rules and he didn't know what to do about that, so finally he said he just gave up and he never talked to her again. She kind of lived there untalked to except for me and Pigg until she was old enough to move out."

"They didn't get on so good."

"Like oil and water."

"What about the two of you?" I asked.

"Oh, I go see Daddy about every eighteen months or so," said Pigg. "Sometimes Mag comes."

"Sometimes not," said Mag.

"Mom always told me he lived too far away to visit," I said.

"Well, we're going. I've decided. Besides, I don't think she meant the distance literally," said Pigg.

"Oh," I said.

So we drove there the next day, not speaking much. I guess the ladies' mouths were dry because they kept taking short nervous sips out of Coke cans the whole way there and not saying anything. And when we finally pulled into the ramshackle piece of land, which was up straight against a mountain, with a tangle of old brush hanging over it like uncombed hair, we got out of the car and a kind of all-bones, stooped, but tall guy came up to me. He was wearing overalls, and his face was sunk in permanent brown wrinkles like a big old basset hound. I could see where Mom got her looks. He glared at me squint-eyed like he wasn't going to like me because my mom had had me, but he put out his hand, so I had to shake it. Pigg said, "Say hello to your granddaddy."

"Least you're a boy," he said to me. "Call me Chet."

So I knew we weren't going to be trying to make up for any lost time. He took me out to see the two old horses he still had.

"Are these the ones that were here when Pigg and Mom and Mag grew up here?" I asked, looking at the horses grazing across the fenced meadow.

"No, these here are different horses," said Chet, leaning on the fence. "I always keep two around." I would have liked to see the horses up closer, but he suddenly swung around on me and barked, "How you do at school, boy?"

I could also see why Mag and Pigg called me "boy." I guess it was a way of talking they grew up with, but after hearing Chet talk I knew they'd all refined their speech since leaving Chet and the backwoods of Kentucky.

"I do pretty good," I said.

"Then what are these two taking you out for? Shouldn't you be in school right now? Or are you like your mama and you think you can just go when you want and stay home when you want?"

So I explained about how it was all my aunts' idea, this vacation, being careful to leave out the part about Mag almost dying in case it wasn't something she wanted to tell him.

"Humph," he said as we headed back alongside the slope of the mountain to his front door. His house had no paint on it and the roof looked like it was about to pour down onto the porch, but other than that he didn't seem to be in such bad circumstances. He had his horses. Looked to me like he had his health, and when I got in he made us all jelly sandwiches and hot cups of tea, so I guess he could cook. I didn't like the tea but drank it anyway because he was a little scary with his humphy disapproval.

"Yep, always had two horses. Done more damage and cost me more money than anything."

"Nobody's making you keep them, Daddy," said Pigg.

Chet ignored this. "I remember one time I was taking my new bay home, walking it back from where I bought it. This was after you girls had left. Hey, you haven't even seen my new horses!" he said suddenly, putting his hands on the arms of his chair to hoist himself into a half-standing position.

"Sit back down, Daddy," said Mag. "We don't want to see your horses."

"I should have had boys. These girls would never have known a stallion from a nag. Broke my heart how little interest they had. So I was bringing back this bay who was young and green and I had him on the road on a lead, down there by St. Mary's Church, in the middle of nowheres, really. Just a church on one side of the road and a bus stop across from it, a good mile or so from town. And a bus stops suddenly and the horse fair goes nuts. He's spooking all over the road. He goldurn runs right over this foot. Now, it's one thing, boy, to have a horse step on your foot. I've been stepped on plenty when I was too stupid to watch out, but when you're on asphalt and a horse is running and you get the whole 1,200 pounds grinding your little pinkie toe into the dust, which is what happened, well, let me tell you, you're goin' make some noise. So I'm tryin' to hang on to the lead and hopping on one foot and swearing fit to beat the band and a woman gets off the bus and stands there watching me like a goldurn idiot and the bus takes off again, so the horse is spooking, and I'm screaming and hopping. This idiot woman starts walking up to me and I think, well, she's not a total retardo, she's goin' see what she can do for me, and you know what she says when she gets up to me?"

There was a silence as Chet waited for our answers,

but we didn't have any, which didn't seem to surprise him.

"She says, 'There any place to eat around here?' Now, I ask you, what kind of a question is that to ask a man 'bout to be killed by a runaway horse?"

"What'd you say, Daddy?" asked Pigg.

"Well, that's the stupidest thing yet. 'Stead of telling her where to go, or turning that wild horse free to run over *her* foot, see how *she* likes it, I find myself saying between my yells, 'There's a café down the road a piece in town.' But does that get rid of her?"

He waited for our replies, but we were a little short on answers that day.

"No, it does not. She looks at me all disappointed like, like I should've done better than that and she must protest. 'Oh, that's too far. I've got a funeral in an hour.' And she pauses like *I'm* supposed to feel sorry for *her*. 'And I don't want to walk all the way into town. Isn't there someplace closer?' Well, we both look down the road, like we can't see nothing but fields for miles in either direction, and then I just say 'No' and she gives this little shrug like I done it to her on purpose. Like maybe I should have invited her over for a goldurn cheese sammich or somethin'. What do you think of that, boy?"

Well, the trouble was, I liked his story but I could never like a father who hadn't talked to his daughter since she was thirteen, especially as the daughter was my mother, so I decided to look bored by the whole business, and a look of disappointment crossed his face that made me feel a bit sleazy about hurting him, but I thought, What does he care what I think? But I guessed he didn't often have people to tell things to. Then Pigg and Mag stood up.

"Well, as usual, you just get here and you leave, you just get here and leave," he said, not bothering to stand up.

"We gotta go, Daddy," said Pigg.

"Uh-huh," said Chet.

Nobody bothered to kiss each other goodbye or anything. This was not a kissy family. Pigg and Mag and I got in the car and Pigg turned the car around in the yard. I looked out the back window to see Chet not even looking at us but staring across the border.

Florida

WHAT HAPPENED NEXT was maybe the strangest thing ever that happened on this trip. Pigg wanted to see the Everglades. By and large we had been following Mag's nose up to this point, going where she wanted, but Mag had been gaining weight steadily and with it some of her mortal strength, and she had begun splitting the driving with Pigg. That and having for once chosen the destination—going to see Chet—had made Pigg realize that this was her trip, too.

"And I would like to go down into the mangrove deeps," she said to Mag. They'd both picked up their father's Kentucky drawl, so different from their civilized Virginian way of speaking.

"Aren't we being a tad dramatic, Pigg?" asked Mag.

So we drove and drove, days and part of nights now that we had two drivers, although Mag kept reminding us that we had no agenda.

At some point while we were on our way to Florida someone found my mother, but the phone call about this was extremely unsatisfying, as our cell kept breaking up.

Mag answered the phone first, languidly pulling it out of her purse. We'd been off in our own little worlds for the last two hours of driving and she was clearly thinking of something else at the time and seemed surprised to find herself speaking to my mother. "KATHERINE?" she said, coming back to the here and now with a crash. "My God. Just a second." And she handed the phone wordlessly to me.

"Mom?" I said, and I'm embarrassed to say my voice shook.

"I am found!" This reminded me of that line in "Amazing Grace," and I couldn't get it out of my head for the rest of the phone call. It gave kind of a redemptive feeling to the whole thing, which I am sure was unintentional on the part of my mother and would have surprised her a good deal.

"Who found you?"

"Well, Daddy, of course," said my mother, always one to spread the credit around. "Where are . . . crackle crackle crackle hiss hiss."

"Mom, the phone is breaking up, I can't hear you. The phone is breaking up. Mom? Mom?"

Then I heard my father saying, "I can't fix their cell

phone, Katherine. For heaven's . : . hello? Hello? Son? We found your mother!"

Well, I mean, really. Duh.

"Where did you find her?" Then more crackles and hisses, which we waited out.

"In the jungle!"

Double duh and more hisses and crackles.

"I can barely hear you, son, and it sounds like you're someplace far from a cell tower. But your mother is . . ."

More crackles. More hisses. It was really agony at this point.

"She's what? Dad? Mom is what?" I shouted.

"Fine," said Dad's voice, clear as a bell because the connection was back.

"Well, thank goodness for that," I said.

"How's the trip?" asked Dad as if my mother's being lost in the jungle was a mere peccadillo. Sometimes his priorities were extremely mixed up.

"Well, who found her? How?"

"Tourists kept spotting her. You'd be amazed at the number of tourists in the Ugandan jungle," he said.

"Really?" I said. "I wouldn't have thought."

"Yes, quite a revelation. Quite. Of course, they had guides."

"Yes, I guess they would," I said.

"She and the student kept trying to hook up with tourists because they would spot them with their binoculars but then they'd lose them, and they figured as long as they stayed with the chimps, the primatologists would find the chimps, and then the primatologists would find *them*. So they just followed the monkeys, son." Crackle crackle, long hissss, and the phone appeared to go dead. But then the connection came back suddenly and I heard my mother shouting, "Helllooooo? Are you there?"

"It was a smart move on your part," I said. "Following those monkeys!"

"Well, your father isn't so sure. He says it was stupid to get lost in the first place."

"He was just worried," I said, beginning to sound worried myself. "Anyone can get lost."

"Your father says that if I followed the rules the guide laid out, then I never would have gone after that monkey and gotten lost . . . actually, it was a chimp."

It reminded me of a conversation my father had with me once when he took me fishing on Cushinaw Lake. "There's a right way and a wrong way to bait a hook," he said, rebaiting mine the right way.

"Are you sure?" I asked because the way I was doing it was working fine for me.

"There's a right way and a wrong way to do everything. Of course, you're going to have to learn your own right and wrong to hold to, because that will be your moral compass, son. And with a moral compass you need never get lost, and believe me, we're all afraid of getting lost."

{ 95 }

I wasn't afraid of any such thing at the time. We were right in the middle of Cushinaw Lake, but my father nodded several times like he'd delivered a particularly juicy bit of advice this time. I nodded, too, not because I knew what he meant but just 'cause I liked my dad and it felt good, the two of us nodding together, out in the middle of the lake. I guess as far as he was concerned, my mother had found the wrong way to be in the jungle.

Then the phone went dead and didn't ring again and we didn't know where to call my parents, but when we crossed the state line going into Florida I went in with considerable relief of mind, which was a good thing because of what was to follow.

Pigg decided she wanted to camp. We drove down to Turtle Creek, where Pigg had read there were mangrove swamps. People were real friendly. Whenever someone found out we wanted to camp, they told us about all the great parks and the great beaches, but they got very quiet when Pigg told them we weren't interested in beaches. We wanted to camp by a big old swamp. There would always be a thinking pause and then the person would ask why. I guess during the thinking pause they were trying to figure it out for themselves but they always came up empty. "If you've seen one beach, you've seen them all," Mag would answer, and this would generally shut them up except for one storeowner who said, "I'd say if you'd seen one *swamp*, you'd seen them all," and I thought, Good for him.

We were staying in motels while we acquired all the paraphernalia for this big adventure, and it really seemed to excite Pigg. We went into camping outfitters and bought things like pup tents (which turned out to be very important to me in the weeks to come) and sleeping bags and a little cookstove. Pigg bought quite a few collapsible cups—it seems she had a real thing for them—and air mattresses so we could float through the swamp, even though people kept telling Pigg that you should never go in the water; it was full of poisonous snakes, alligators, *and* crocodiles for Pete's sake. Turned out those swamps were the only place in the world where both alligators and crocodiles lived, which made them sound like *especially* bad swamps, and the locals seemed to take pride in that. But really, none of us could tell an alligator from a crocodile, so it was much of a muchness to us. And Pigg just said piffle. She'd never seen either an alligator or a crocodile and she didn't expect she'd be lucky enough to see one in the near future. I have noticed that there are certain bad things that everyone just decides from the beginning are never going to happen to *them*, and alligators and crocodiles seemed to be on Pigg's list.

Pigg bought what she thought would be good camp food: peanut butter and jelly and Wonder bread, potato chips, and graham crackers, marshmallows, and Hershey chocolate bars for s'mores.

"Some less," said Mag acidly. She was beginning to fill out after all those big meals on the road. "Why are you buying things that you would never buy at home, and who do you think is going to eat this food?"

"This is camp food," said Pigg happily. Nobody was going to rain on her camping parade.

"Are we eschewing our dainty salads and mineral water this week?"

"No, dear," said Pigg. "I'm buying this for you."

"*Me?* Well, I can't eat all this, and neither can the boy."

"Sure you can, Mag, you've been eating like you've got a dozen intestines ever since we started this trip."

After that they didn't talk to each other for a day and a half, until we were actually setting up our campsite on Turtle Creek. We had our own dock and a nice patch of green from which we could see the swamp.

"What I don't understand," I said, "is why those people say we can't possibly float in the swamp but it's perfectly okay to camp alongside it. Can't alligators and crocodiles crawl up onshore and eat you just as easily while you're sleeping?"

"Well, exactly," said Pigg. "And do you think they would even *have* campsites here if that had ever happened? Trust me, the alligators and crocodiles, *if* they exist, are more afraid of you than you are of them. Besides, they've got plenty to eat in the swamp, why bother coming up onshore? This is all protected land, you know, and there's lots of things for reptiles to chomp away on."

"Not to mention all this p.b. and j.," said Mag drily, and then they were talking again.

And so we spent three days in tents being very nasty to each other because there really wasn't that much to do and Pigg was the only one enamored with swamp life. She had bought a pair of binoculars and kept them trained on the far jungly shore, hoping to see Lord knows what. I had run out of reading material, and when they admonished me for not stocking up with more at our last mall bookstore stop, I reminded them that no one had said we were going to spend three days or more at the swamp, and went and got my inflatable raft, blew it up, and climbed on it. I was angry and desperate or I never would have done it, because I believed very strongly in poisonous snakes and alligators, no matter what Pigg said.

I floated down the creek watching the sky and the pelicans for a while, and then I rolled onto my stomach and let the creek take me lazily along. I drifted past the campgrounds and onward to where people had their own small homes and docks. A boy who had been playing onshore in front of his house suddenly walked into the creek, lay on his back, and floated ahead of me. Now, I really wasn't afraid because I figured if locals got in the water without even benefit of air mattresses, then all these stories of alligators were just to frighten the tourists away, the way people in Maine are always supposed to give tourists the wrong directions. People do mean things.

Well, I floated unconcernedly for a while until it occurred to me that me and this boy were going kind of far afield. The houses had disappeared and we had only mangrove around us and then the creek narrowed and the boy stood up, walked to the edge of it, and started wading into the deep bushy swamp. I started to follow, to say, hey, where are you going, bubs, that doesn't look smart to me, when a sharp root sticking up out of the water pierced my raft. I felt I was in for it then because even if this boy knew there were no alligators, it seemed to me it always paid to be on the safe side and I wanted the benefit of my protective air mattress.

"HEY! HEY!" I called after the boy because now it occurred to me that I didn't want to be this far down the creek in the middle of nowhere without my local guide. I didn't know the ins and outs of this darn swamp and I was mad at Pigg for having suggested it in the first place, and because I was already mad I allowed myself to take it one step further and get mad at Mag because one of things she had said after my mother's phone call was that she knew my mother would be fine because selfish people always were. Between her and Chet, I'd had just about enough Mom-trashing for one week, and I was fuming over this and yelling to the boy, but he didn't answer and then it occurred to me that maybe he was deaf. I was scratched and frightened by the time I caught up with him, now with water to our waists and bushes everywhere, and night was falling and I was thinking, Jeez, I hope he knows where's he's going, I hope there's a town at the end of this shortcut he's taking. "Hey!" I said again as he turned and looked at me, and then my stomach dropped because his eyes were empty and I realized I was lost in a mangrove swamp with a boy who wasn't all there and hadn't any idea where he was either, only he didn't seem to mind, so I guess, because of that, for that moment in that swamp he was the luckier one.

Now, you may not believe this, but I followed that boy down that creek for three days more. Having no choice. He never spoke a word but at night would float on the current, singing little tuneless ditties. Something that was going on in his head, no doubt, which I had no clue or key to. We did see alligators and crocodiles, too, I guess, and lots of snakes and even more fish, and at night the arms of those mangroves seemed frightening, like trolls sinking into the miry waters. I wanted to hightail and run every time I saw one of the fearsome reptiles that would eat us alive soon as blink, but that boy didn't seem to mind them at all and would more than likely stand transfixed, studying a spider, while large-toothed creatures passed, and I had no choice but to hold still, too, or go off alone, which I sure as heck wasn't doing, and maybe that's what saved us because the crocodiles always glided on by, out for livelier food perhaps but not seeming to notice us standing like statues, one all absorbed in a spider, the other quietly hyperventilating onshore.

One night we had a thunderstorm that rocked the mangrove; lightning flashed, illuminating the night mysteries of the swamp. And it's funny, now I wasn't afraid of the lightning, it was so beautiful, and I even liked the sound of the thunder because at least it was something familiar, but the boy nearly went out of his head every time it flashed. "Don't worry," I'd say to him, "it's just a little lightning. I've seen worse in Virginia." He hadn't said a word to me yet; I don't know if he even knew any. Maybe not, because he sure didn't take comfort from any of mine, and I guess it made the night kind of long for him. That was the only night we stayed still, huddled onshore; the rest of the time he seemed to prefer to keep moving, which was a good idea, scared or no. But later, when we were moving by daylight, I thought how funny it was that we were frightened by such different things, him of the lightning and me of the swamp creatures, and yet we were neither of us hurt, not counting the endless scratches and bug bites. We were so tired out after the night of the thunderstorm that it felt like we'd always be going down that creek, and that didn't seem so bad. It was almost as if, if I could be here, I mean be here and be okay, then I could be anywhere, it didn't really matter, and if I could be anywhere, I could never really be lost.

And so we plugged on. Then on the fourth morning the air changed and I felt like I tasted salt in my mouth. The water got deeper and we were floating on down a little faster, and sometimes I'd panic that the current would pull us in different directions or my bathing trunks would get caught on a branch the way his had once, and that off he would go, drifting away, him to his fate and me to mine, and I wasn't ready for that, not yet. He had no trunks to catch on things anymore, they'd been ripped off by a root the day before and no point rescuing as they were in shreds anyway. He floated on naked down the creek, not seeming to mind or even notice, so we must have looked a sight to the man in the motor boat calmly fishing when the creek finally opened up to the sea and there we were. He pulled the boy in first and then me and said, "Well, golly gee. Well, don't this beat all? You must be Henry and this is that autistic kid, Jeremiah, ain't it? Is that who you are? What am I saying? Of course that's who you are. Who else would you be? I've seen Jeremiah's picture on the TV. They've been looking for you boys."

"Yeah, I guess that's us," I said. I was a little short of words. I had, after all, been floating through a swamp for three days.

"We gotta get you off to the police. The papers have

been full of you. They thought you were dead. Green Berets out looking for you. You look about dead."

I didn't know what to say. Clearly, whatever else we were, we weren't dead.

"You saved this here boy, Henry. You're going to be a hero!" he said. "No way he could have come through that swamp without you."

"Actually," I said, "it wasn't like that at all. I just followed him."

"You *saved* him," he said.

"Not really," I said.

"Did you see swamp critters? Gators and such?"

"Lots," I said.

"However did you protect yourself and this one? That's what I'd like to know. The Lord above must have been watching over you."

"Well, sure, of course," I said, because a guy like that, coming along in a boat, with a different take on events, the least you can do is be agreeable, people *will* put their own spin on things, and besides I was hoping he maybe had a sandwich with him somewhere. "The truth is, we just seemed to keep going until we got here and I was really following him."

"Now, don't you go telling folks *that* story," said the man. "No, it's your chance to be a *hero*, boy. Anyone who comes out of that swamp alive would be, but you got more cause than most because you brung this feller with you. No, you're a hero. Why, I'll attest to that. You want me to tell them newspaper fellers that when I came upon you, you were carrying this here feller in your arms? Like a sack of potatoes?"

"No, thank you," I said, horrified. This was getting worse and worse.

"That's what I think I *will* tell them. Now listen to me. There might even be some reward money in it for you, though not from this feller's mother, she's poor as a church mouse, though she'll be heaps grateful to you."

"Please stop," I said.

That seemed to tick him off, but I didn't have the energy for longer explanations, and he didn't talk to me the rest of the way. We banked his boat and got into an old beat-up Chevy convertible and rode to the police station, a ragged dirty beach towel wrapped modestly around Jeremiah, who didn't seem any more happy or unhappy than he had been in the swamp. In the police station we sat and ate doughnuts and I waited for Mag and Pigg to pick me up, which they did shortly. The police wanted me to go to the hospital, but I said I felt fine, just real, real tired, and I wanted so much simply to go home, and then I realized I didn't have a home per se—we were on vacation. Mag and Pigg had packed up all the camping stuff and had been staying in a motel during the search for us. They hadn't notified my parents because they didn't know how to reach them and had no news to tell them anyway. And we decided that we wouldn't tell them about this, at least not yet.

The police reluctantly let me go, and we got out of there as the newspaper people started arriving. One of them grabbed on to me and asked me if I was Henry the swamp boy, and I said no. We ran for the car and got away and I fell asleep in the backseat thinking about the boat man and how he was going to give them his own version of what happened and how it didn't matter to me, I just wanted to get out of Florida.

"Was it so horrible?" asked Pigg, and I thought about the night watching the lightning cutting through the darkness and the silent boy and the way we just floated on down through the dangers of those waters, and I said truthfully no, though I wouldn't want to do it again for a long while. Then Mag said to Pigg that camping had been a stupid idea to begin with and Pigg said she guessed it was my turn to choose what to do and I said really what I wanted was to be on the road again, driving, driving, and because it was still early in the day that's what we did, and the car was hot, which felt good to me, and I slept and slept in the backseat until nightfall and we parked at a motel and then I slept some more.

The Four Towers

I ROLLED ALONG in the car for three days after that, sleeping day and night. I figured it took as many days to recover from such an adventure as to have it. Pigg and Mag kept saying I was experiencing stress trauma, but really I was just sleepy and hungry. Every so often we would stop for something to eat and I would fill up, same as filling up your car; I had almost no interest in the food apart from getting it down and getting back to sleep. I kept falling asleep with a full belly, thinking this must be what a pregnant woman felt like because my belly, having starved itself for three days, felt stretched out beyond its usual capacities, like a large creature was moving around within it. The evening of the third day we were crossing the border into Arkansas, sitting at a Howard Johnson's table, and the waitress asked for our order. Pigg ordered a large chef's salad, hold the cheese and egg and salad dressing and pretty much everything that made it worth-while, and Mag ordered fried chicken. She was back at her fighting weight, but she just couldn't help herself anymore. She had gotten used to being full and content, and when you're sitting in a car most of the day you don't notice how lumbering you have become. I'm afraid she was headed for obesity. Not that it would bother me. I merely noted its coming. And I ordered a hamburger, fries, and a milk shake, and that's when Mag went crazy. She put a hand up, signaling to the waitress that she was *not* to write down my order.

"You have been ordering hamburgers, french fries, and milk shakes for lunch and dinner ever since we left home. I've had enough. I can't stand it anymore."

"It's perfectly nutritionally sound," I said with equa-nimity. "Almost always there is a piece of lettuce and a slice of tomato on the bun."

"I am not the least concerned about your health," said Mag. "I am concerned about my own intense boredom. I'm telling you, boy, I've had it. Order something else."

"Mag . . ." said Pigg in low tones. She hated a scene even if the only person to witness it was this lone waitress who, anyway, appeared as if she looked forward to watch-ing a tussle.

"Well . . ." I said, opening the menu to study it. I really hadn't had any run-ins so far with either of them and didn't want to start now. My guess was that Mag had tired

The Four Towers

of treating me like a beloved invalid for three days, which they had been doing, so relieved were they to have me back and not have to face the possibility of telling my parents they had carelessly mislaid me. And truth was Mag really liked to be the beloved invalid. My guess was that she would eat her way into such an enormous size she wouldn't be able to move and we'd all be expected to wait hand and foot on her and tell her what a shame it was she was the size of Mount Olympus. "Well . . ." I said.

"Order the clams," said Mag, reaching across the table and snapping my menu closed.

"I don't like clams," I said.

"These clams are fried. They bear no resemblance to clams on the half shell," said Mag. To the waitress she said, "He'll have the clams."

"I don't want clams," I said.

"Have you ever had clams? I bet you've never even tasted a clam."

"Okay," I said, "I haven't, but I don't want them."

"Clams for you," said Mag and that was that. I must say I sat there in a sulk. They had given me crayons and a kids' menu, not noticing how old I was. I wanted to tell them I had, after all, survived three days in a swamp, but now I was glad for the crayons. I sat there and played tic-tac-toe solitaire and ignored Mag completely. Pigg looked nervous and kept taking sips from her Diet Coke and Mag had her eyes squinted and her lips pursed and looked mean and unbending. She opened sugar packets and dumped them one by one into her iced tea until it was practically sherbet. I don't think any of us was having a very good time, which was a shame in a place that served twenty-eight flavors of ice cream.

Eventually our dinners came, and I looked at my plate poutily. Pigg nervously ate a piece of lettuce. I ate a french fry and then another. There was a mound of what looked like fried bits of Kleenex or something on my plate, which is frankly not how I thought a clam would turn out when fried. There was a little cup of tartar sauce, which also looked fairly foul.

"Tartar sauce, yum yum, how lovely," said Pigg.

We didn't say anything. Mag started in on her fried chicken.

"How I wish I could still eat tartar sauce. I gave up tartar sauce a long time ago," said Pigg. We still didn't say anything. "One hundred calories a tablespoon."

"Don't push it, Pigg," said Mag. Then she turned to me. "Stop eating those fries and try a clam."

"Yes, dear, do," said Pigg. "Just to make Mag happy. I'll tell you what, if you don't like them, you can order anything on the menu you do like."

"Except hamburger, fries, and milk shake," said Mag.

I picked one up and put it in my mouth. Then I raised my eyebrows in a most snooty manner and ate another one. Then I tried a little tartar sauce just to round out the experience. Then I put some tartar sauce on my french fries.

"There, now," said Pigg. "You've been more than fair. We'll call the waitress back and you can order something you like."

"Don't bother," I said sulkily, and continued eating.

"No, no, dear, we want you to have a good dinner," said Pigg. "He *did* try one, Mag."

"It's okay," I said, continuing to eat them.

"Really, Henry, you needn't," said Pigg. "Need he, Mag?"

"I said he only had to try them," said Mag, who was eating her own dinner with a great show of unconcern.

"Well then, I'll get the waitress," said Pigg, starting to half rise to signal her.

"I said, it's ALL RIGHT!" I snapped in a loud voice that embarrassed Pigg because several tables turned to look at us.

"Why are you being so difficult?" hissed Pigg.

"Because I LIKE them," I said with exasperation.

There was a silence while the three of us realized what I'd said, and just looked at each other for a minute, and then we started laughing, and once we started we couldn't stop. It wasn't even that funny but we were splitting our sides, tears running down our faces, falling sideways in the booth and pounding the nice red fake leather. I was afraid we would scare people and get tossed out, but the waitress was looking over, smiling indulgently at us. Eventually we all recovered enough to order ice cream, or in Pigg's case, tea.

After she ordered her ice cream Mag went to the ladies' room and on the way back bought a copy of the local paper from the dispenser by the door. At the table she opened it and searched for something concerning the swamp story. We had been following it with interest for three days because I seemed to have disappeared from it entirely. According to the stories, this boy, Jeremiah, had gone down the creek alone. No mention of me at all.

"How can they do that?" I asked Mag and Pigg.

"Reporters can do anything," said Pigg.

"They create their own version of events. That's why I never listen to the news," said Mag.

"But you said I was in all the papers for the three days we were lost, so then how do they explain that suddenly instead of two boys making the trip, only one did?" The funny thing was that they didn't seem to need to explain. There was no mention of anyone ever questioning this, no letter in the paper about it, no, it was like I never existed, one boy more or less didn't matter, it was still a good story, and what happened to Jeremiah was that he became a miracle. Everyone knew no one could get through those glades with those crocodiles and alligators. There were places in those swamps even the Green Berets had never been. So certainly one small boy wasn't going to make it, especially an autistic one. Perhaps his autism saved him, said one article, and then more and more people wrote in saying they thought it was a miracle. A miracle had happened at Turtle Creek! There was a groundswell, and apparently a couple of years down the line the Pope was called in to make it official, and there was a monument put up on the shore where the man in the motorboat had saved us, only he changed his story to finding the one lone naked boy scratched and bleeding and *smiling* with something like divine light, I guess. Well, he was willing to lie about anything, that guy. The only time I remember the boy smiling was when an officer got him a bag of chips out of the vending machine. We were both real hungry.

Well, it brought a lot of tourism to Turtle Creek, and the boy probably never even knew he was a miracle boy, even though people built a shrine on his front lawn and people were always dropping off flowers there and wanting him to touch them.

"Still, all's well that ends well," said Mag. "I take it you didn't want to be a miracle boy."

"No, thank you," I said, spooning into my peppermint stick ice cream.

"Although," said Pigg, who was sitting there with a cup of tea and so had time to think about things, whereas Mag and I were focused on getting the maximum pleasure out of our ice cream, "in a way, you know, you *were* a miracle boy. If you think about it. I mean, the Green Berets said they never expected to find you alive. That they wouldn't bet on their own men coming out alive if they'd been lost in that swamp for three days."

"Well, I don't know if it was a miracle," I said. I didn't tell them that getting out of the swamp didn't seem such a miracle to me, what felt like the miracle was what happened *in* the swamp when I realized I wasn't lost at all. I wondered if my mom had had this same thought at some time and that's why she knew we were all okay every minute, all the time. But I lied because I thought it was a better idea to pretend to keep thinking like a normal person. "Mostly just lucky. I mean, we *had* to keep going. There was nothing else to do *except* keep going. But it could have just as easily ended badly, it seems to me."

"Seems to me, too," said Mag through a mouthful of sundae. She was going all out. Pigg frowned at her. I think her eating habits were beginning to annoy Pigg. "I guess you believe anything that doesn't end badly is a miracle," she said in response to Pigg's frown.

This really teed Pigg off.

The next morning we drove until we found a mall, and Pigg and Mag took me to a bookstore and loaded me up with books. It was the last act of guilt obeisance I was to receive from them over the whole swamp thing, so I made the most of it. After all, they really should have watched me better. Then Pigg said that it was my turn to decide where to go, which was how I knew Mag was done with guilt because she said that this was ridiculous, I was only eleven (she never got my age right once on this trip), and how would I know what I wanted to see? But, actually, being in Louisiana had put an idea in my head, and I said I wanted to see my father's cousins' House of Four Towers.

"What in the world is that?" asked Pigg.

"I told you not to let him pick, Pigg," said Mag.

"What's wrong with going to see the four towers?" I asked. Actually I didn't care all that much. I was happy going anywhere as long as I had a big pile of books, but they had said I could pick, so then they should let me pick. Fair was fair.

My father told me that his cousins Chuck and Lulu built a house that had not one tower but four: one on each side of the house like a castle. It's somewhere in Louisiana, and I always wanted to see it.

"Oh dear, I remember them from your parents' wedding," said Pigg. "Don't you, Mag?"

"No," said Mag, getting out a map. "Let's go to the museum of lard in Little Rock."

"They named their youngest something really weird, what was it?" said Pigg.

"Puppy," Mag said. "Their kids are called Nadine and Puppy."

"Oh, right," said Pigg, sighing.

I knew the story behind this, too, because my father told me when he told me about the house with the four towers. Apparently Lulu and Chuck had a hard time getting pregnant, and then right before they finally did, they decided it would never happen, so they better just get a puppy, and so when the next day they found out Lulu was pregnant they decided to name the baby Puppy.

"I suspect he was beaten up every day of his life," said Mag.

"How old must he be now, Mag?" asked Pigg.

"Teens, maybe early twenties. How could you forget a name like Puppy?" asked Mag.

"Oh, I don't know, hormones," said Pigg worriedly.

Mag made a snorting noise. "You're too young for hormones." Pigg was three years younger than Mag. She didn't seem old at all, but as she drove along she kept looking worried and asked Mag continually if she looked like she had gotten a *lot* older in the last few years, and then finally when we had pulled into the motel and settled, she got into the car alone and said she wanted to go do some shopping, which was downright weird, leaving Mag and me stranded in a crummy motel room on a stretch of lonely road, so I set up the pup tent in the room. I could just fit it, slightly less than completely expanded, in a corner of the room, and I took the mattress off my ever-present cot and dove in there with a flashlight and read. I think Mag and I were both glad for the privacy, and when Pigg came back she had cut her hair short and had it spiked and dyed blond. The little blond spikes stuck up all over her head.

"Oh my heavens," said Mag, throwing up her hands.

I had no opinion at all, but Pigg seemed happy. So the next day we set out to find the House of Four Towers. It didn't occur to me until we were driving on down toward the bayous that Pigg was as strange a name as Puppy, after all. I had gotten so used to calling Aunt Pigg, Pigg that it no longer seemed strange. Probably Puppy didn't seem odd to Chuck and Lulu and Nadine either. I was glad we had driven down to the deep, dark bayous of Louisiana because it was like no place we had been up until then. Trees hung with Spanish moss like the whole of southern Louisiana was some frowsty old Victorian parlor, hung with shredding draperies. I expected to get out and find the air full of death and must, but it was pretty ordinary air, I have to admit.

"Now, where do they live. Where *do* they live?" Pigg kept asking herself when we had finally gotten down to the general vicinity. "If we only had our computer, we could go on people search and get their address. They mentioned where they were from at the wedding, but that was so long ago I can't remember where it was, can you, Mag?"

"No, Armpit, Arkansas, something like that," said Mag, lazily flipping pages in a *People* magazine. She wanted nothing to do with this little venture and had been against it from the start, as she kept reminding us every twenty miles or so.

"No, it was definitely Louisiana," said Pigg. "I know, give me the phone, Mag, I'll call the office and get one of the kids to see if they can locate them on the Internet."

That's when we found out the cell phone wasn't working. Mag and Pigg didn't seem all that distressed at first, just annoyed at the inconvenience, but then they didn't have parents in Africa.

"Don't you get it, what if Dad and Mom have been trying to reach us?" I squawked.

"Now, that *is* a problem, Henry," said Pigg, sighing and pulling over to the side of the road.

"And this is the only way they can!" I yelled. "And we don't have a number for them."

"Calm down," said Mag, who never did like a crisis or people leaping around unless it was her. She put her magazine down and pulled her sunglasses to the tip of her nose. "We'll just go into town and buy a new cell phone and call the office. If your parents couldn't reach us on this one, I'm sure they would call there next to find out if we had checked in to say, for instance, that our cell phone had died. You're sure it's not just the batteries, Pigg?"

"No, no, it was perfectly recharged. Besides, listen to it, Mag, it's on but it's making that awful fuzzy sound."

"Well, maybe we're out of range of a cell tower," said Mag.

"No, it's broken," said Pigg, shaking her head sadly. "I feel it in my bones."

"That's not the type of thing people feel in their bones," said Mag, and they argued about what types of things people can feel in their bones all the way to Baton Rouge.

In Baton Rouge we got a new cell phone and Pigg called the office to check on Lulu and Chuck's whereabouts. They lived in a little town called Petunia, Louisiana. "Isn't that precious?" said Mag, who could be quite unpleasant when she didn't get her way.

"Oh, and by the way, honey," said Pigg to whichever assistant was aiding her, "we didn't get a call from Norman or Katherine, did we? We what? You what? Oh no. Did they leave a number? No number. As usual. What is the matter with those people? Going where? I see. Okay. Well, here's the new cell phone number. Give it to them the next time they phone in, will you?"

Pigg turned to us in dismay. We were sitting in the car, parked along a curb, eating hamburgers from a drive-in and watching Baton Rouge strut by.

"Okay, we've got a problem," said Pigg, and took a hamburger out of the bag, slowly unwrapped it, and munched it contemplatively. "Yep, I'd say a definite problem."

"What's that?" asked Mag, looking unconcernedly out the window. Ever since we had insisted on seeing the House of Four Towers she'd affected the air of someone who really didn't care *what* happened to her next.

"Well, Norman and Katherine tried to call us, to tell us they were going down the east coast of Africa to chill out on the beaches, and when they couldn't get ahold of us, they called our office and a girl in the office had seen a story about Henry's disappearance on CNN, but when *she* tried to get ahold of us she couldn't either, of course. Then there were the follow-up stories about one boy coming out of the swamp and no mention of Henry, so she told Norman and Katherine all this and they called the Turtle Creek police, who said that Henry had disappeared but also been found and we had taken him and no one knew where we were and Katherine and Norman are fit to be tied. As you can imagine."

"Umm," said Mag, licking ketchup off her fingers. "Katherine's not going to be very pleasant, is she?"

"No, on the whole I'd say not," said Pigg.

"Well, it serves her right. Now she knows how it feels, family members getting themselves lost all over the place with no concern for others. Anyhow, who cares, she'll call the office back, get the new cell phone number, we'll explain things, and that will be that."

"Hmm," said Pigg, and started up the car again.

"And, Pigg," said Mag smugly.

"Yes?"

"You ate a hamburger."

Pigg looked with dismay at the empty wrapper on her lap. "Gosh-darn it!" she said. She looked in the bag, and there was the salad she had ordered, untouched.

"But go ahead and have the salad, too," said Mag. "I don't want it. I'm *quite* full."

"I didn't mean to eat your second hamburger, Mag," said Pigg as we drove out of Baton Rouge and headed for Petunia.

"No, but you did," said Mag happily.

• • •

We reached the house with the four towers by late afternoon. Mag had Chuck and Lulu's phone number, so she phoned ahead to let them know we were on our way. Lulu said, "Oh," and then, "How wonderful, you must stay with us." But Mag said there was just a little too long of a pause between the "Oh" and the "How wonderful," and besides, she'd rather stay in a motel. So when we arrived we were greeted more effusively than we might otherwise have been, said Mag from the front seat, putting on her company face.

"Mag! Pigg! And this must be Norman's son, Henry!" said Lulu, running down the steps and out to the car. I had imagined the house buried in a bayou with trees and

Spanish moss and maybe another swamp, but it was just in a regular old suburb among other very ordinary split-level-type houses, where it stuck out like a bad idea.

"You must stay the night!" said Lulu before any of us could greet her properly.

"No, no, we couldn't," said Pigg, sounding not very firm. So then Lulu said, "Of course, we don't really have company accommodations, and I really didn't plan to have anyone over to the house until our renovations were finished."

"Oh, what are you doing?" asked Mag. "I don't know if you remember, but Pigg and I are decorators."

"Are you, dear?" said Lulu. "Well, that's very nice, I'm sure. We're redoing our bathrooms and the kitchen and putting in some new floors, and I want to paint the living room. There's always something new to do. We haven't had anyone in to see the house yet, but someday we will."

"You haven't had anyone in since you started the renovations?" said Pigg pleasantly as we sat on the front porch.

"No, dear, since we built it. Well, there's always something to do in a house, isn't there? And I've always been house-proud. My mother used to call me Miss Tidy. Now you sit and I'll get our drinks."

"Let me help you," said Pigg.

"No!" said Lulu. "We'll just all relax out here, shall we? I'll just be a minute."

Lulu went inside, and Mag crossed her eyes at Pigg

and me and said, "They haven't let anyone into the house since it was built—and that was before Henry was born?"

"Sssh," said Pigg because we could hear Lulu heading back to the porch. Pigg leaped up to open the door for her, and she came out with a tray with pieces of walnut cake and a pitcher of lemonade.

"Well, it's a shame you can't stay the night," said Lulu. "After all, a hotel room can never really be like home, can it?"

I thought back to our newly redecorated house with its burnt orange walls and thought home wasn't really like home either. The only place I felt comfortable anymore was the car. If anyone asked me where I was from, I decided I would say, "The car."

"Puppy and Nadine are still working. They both have jobs at the IHOP after school," said Lulu as we loaded our bodies up with sugar.

"Ah," said Pigg, who appeared to be trying to mash up her cake and spread it around her plate so it would look eaten.

"Ah," said Mag. We sort of swung our feet from the rocking chairs, rocking and eating and picking crumbs off our forks. It should have been nice to sit on that porch after being cooped up in the car all day, but Lulu was making it feel all uncomfortable, like she was watching us to make sure we didn't go into the house and maybe steal a glance at things in their imperfect condition. Chuck had come out and waved hello and then gone into the garage or his workshop, as he called it, where he was building a kayak. This was a bit odd, too. Maybe he thought *he* was in imperfect condition. Lulu said it had to be done by Saturday because they were all going kayaking down the bayous. They were part of some church kayaking club.

"Have you ever been in a kayak, Henry?" Lulu asked. She asked me most of the questions because, I think, I was the only one directly related to her, which meant that I was the only one she was actually called upon to show hospitality to. Anyhow, that's how it began to feel to me, and I bet it felt that way to Pigg and Mag, too. It created great pressure for me. I think Mag was enjoying this. She never took her sunglasses off the whole time we were there. Not once.

"No," I said.

"I always taught my children to say 'no, ma'am,' " said Lulu.

"I never liked to be ma'amed, myself," said Mag. "It always made me feel a hundred years old."

"Now, Henry, have you ever been down the bayous? I sure am sorry the kayak isn't ready. It would be lovely to take you for a little trip in it. Of course, I don't enjoy it much myself."

"You don't enjoy it?" said Pigg. "So do you stay home while the others go on the bayou?"

"No, no, no, good heavens no. Of course we all use our kayaks. Chuck likes to make them, and if you make them, you have to use them. It is such a healthy, *clean* form of recreation, don't you think? Now, Henry, have you ever been on the bayous?"

She tilted her head at me inquiringly until I realized I'd never answered her question. "No, I've never been on a bayou," I said. She obviously didn't watch CNN. I couldn't tell the difference between a swamp and a bayou, except that one had a fancy name, but I didn't feel like arguing about it now. She raised her eyebrows, no doubt waiting for me to add "ma'am," which I sure as heck wasn't going to do. "Although I've heard of them, of course," I added to fill the inquiring silence.

"Yes. Your daddy loved the bayous."

"Really?" I said.

"Oh yes. He used to visit us before he married your mother. So, now on the phone Pigg mentioned that they were in Africa. Doing what, if I may be so bold?"

"Missionary work," I said. And then hated myself because I knew I'd only said that because it was clearly the type of thing that would get them brownie points with her, and what did I care about her brownie points?

"*Missionary* work?" said Lulu. "But your daddy has

never been religious. I suppose Katherine got him into that?" She tilted her head at Mag this time. She was like a bird badly in need of a chiropractor.

"It was certainly all Katherine's idea," agreed Mag. "Could I have some more of this lovely cake?"

"I'm sure none of us want more cake, with dinner so soon. I've planned an early dinner because we want to eat it on the porch before the bugs get too bad and I figure, after a long day on the road, you'll want an early evening. Now, I have a few things in the house to do, so you just relax and talk among yourselves and I'll be back in a bit." Then Lulu got up, gathered the cups and plates, and went into the house.

"That woman is intolerable. Intolerable," began Mag, and then her cell phone rang.

Mag handed the phone to me. It was my mother calling to tell me my father had malaria. "Of course, when he heard about the swamp the plan was to fly back immediately to wherever you were. He's very mad at Mag and Pigg. And a little mad at me, too, I'm afraid. He said he told me you were too young to leave for so long. Anyhow, the thing is, we can't go anywhere until his fever goes down. He'd really like Mag and Pigg to take you straight home."

"But I'm fine. And I'm on vacation," I said.

"I know. Oh well, nothing he can do about it now, he's

about out of his mind with fever, so I guess I won't be hearing much more about it for a while."

"Do you want to talk to Mag or Pigg?" I asked.

"No, dear, and I better hang up. Our phone bills are going to be horrendous. On top of everything else."

After that Puppy and Nadine came home and helped Lulu set up card tables on the front porch for dinner, which was very odd because there was no privacy and it was like flaunting your dinner in front of the whole neighborhood.

All during dinner I was worried about malaria. But Mag and Pigg kept telling me it wasn't so bad. People got it all the time from mosquito bites, and people who lived in the West made way too big a deal out of these things.

"To those Africans, why it's just like we think of the common cold," said Mag. " 'Oh, got a bit of malaria to-day,' they say to each other. No big deal."

"I hope he doesn't turn all yellow," said Lulu. Nadine and Puppy were sitting mostly silently through dinner. They seemed like very strange teenagers without much to say, and Chuck was no better unless you were talking about his boat. "My, my, it's a horrible scary thing to have a *disease* in the family, isn't it?"

"And the second one in a month," I said. I don't know why I kept saying these types of things to Lulu. Something about her apparent disapproval made me want to keep confiding things to her, as if I could get her on my side this way. I would make a wonderful hostage.

"Oh?" she said, tilting her head and giving me the beady-eyed inquiring look.

"Mag was sick. She got a funny blood thing," I said. I couldn't tell what Mag was thinking. She was looking in my direction, but her sunglasses were on. I could see from the expression on Pigg's face that I should just shut up.

"Kind of a sickly little family, aren't you?" was all Lulu said, and went back to chomping her catfish. We all ate quietly for a while and Lulu kept passing around rutabagas, mainly because no one seemed to like them. Finally, because the silence was driving me wild, it was so uncomfortable, and I felt this whole part of the trip was my fault, I said, "Tell me about the towers. Why you built four towers?"

"It was very simple really," said Lulu, sitting up straighter and folding her hands in her lap as if she were preparing a posture for storytelling. "You see, we had the opportunity to build our own home. So we picked a design with a tower because I'd always wanted a tower room. But then we all fought so much over who got the tower room for a bedroom, even Puppy and Nadine, who were just four and five, that finally Chuck says, Why don't we each get our own tower room? And it's worked out just fine for us, as we can retire there evenings and really never have to be bothered with each other."

That was the last thing that was said at dinner. Afterward we got away from that house as fast as we could. I couldn't explain what was so horrible about it all, but somehow all four of them had made a mess of things and it was the kind of mess you just wanted to distance yourself from, it was so clearly *their* intimate mess. It left a bad taste on your tongue and we drove as fast and as long as we could without talking about it, right through the night, right under those Louisiana shooting stars, which fled across the sky, too, maybe getting a look at that house and moving on to another part of the sky.

Texas

"**WHERE WOULD YOU ALL LIKE TO GO?**" asked Pigg the next morning, brushing her blond spikes and sitting on the corner of the motel bed where we had finally landed after I had fallen asleep. I vaguely remembered being shaken awake and landing in a cot and wondering how they had gotten it in the motel room so fast. "Would you all like to go to Valley Forge, because I sure would."

"Valley Forge?" said Mag. "Isn't that in, like, Pennsylvania or something?"

"Wouldn't that be fun, Henry, Valley Forge?"

I noticed I was always being enlisted as the swing vote.

"So much history. I've always wanted to see the place where all those men met those chilly deaths. You know, Washington crossing the Potomac and everyone freezing and starving. It was so miserable. I'd just like to take a look and kind of see if you could soak up the misery, get a feel for the place. So much history there. So fascinating. What makes men able to stand being at war?"

We thought about it but finally decided that Texas was a lot closer.

Texas was real big. You got a sense of that right away. And I loved it. I loved the big flat emptiness of it. That was one thing I learned on this trip: some people go for showy mountains and ocean, but what made my heart sing was to see nothing all the way to the horizon. Although Pigg and Mag probably couldn't tell because I lay as usual sprawled along the backseat of the car with my head on some pillows that Mag had bought me at a Kmart for this purpose, watching Texas out the window, mile after mile of empty dustness. It was heaven. It was so unearthly, so unendingly beautiful that I decided that that's what I wanted to do for the rest of my life, just drive through Texas.

Of course, we didn't just drive. We made stops at the museum of knots and a place where there was supposed to be a whole town made out of toothpicks, and when we recommenced driving, I'd be torn between thinking about what I'd just seen and knowing I should be opening my schoolbooks—I was getting way behind—but wanting to either remember where we had been and think about that or think about where we were going or just look out at what was there right now or the emptiness of what wasn't. In the middle of all this thought, every now and then Pigg and Mag made me get out for meal stops. I kept begging for more Howard Johnson's and fried clams, but they kept stopping for barbecue. Once they stopped for Mexican food, and mine was so hot that I said I wouldn't even come out of the car if they tried that again. Unlike the rest of the family, I rarely made these kinds of flat-out refusals, but that hot Mexican food drove me to it. I swear.

"I feel just like Thelma and Louise," said Pigg for the umpteenth time as we drove with windows wide open, a bandanna keeping her hair in place. "Don't you feel just like Thelma and Louise?"

"I do, Pigg, I sure do," said Mag. And I remembered it always because it was one of the few times the two of them agreed on anything.

All the while something kept nagging in the back of my mind the way things do. Something I had heard earlier in the day but hadn't bothered to stop and figure out. Then I had it. Even I knew that Washington crossed the Delaware, not the Potomac. That the Potomac was *in* Washington. I wondered if it was a slip of the tongue or if maybe this design business the two of them talked about working so hard to build on spit was so important to them because they hadn't ever thought they could make much of themselves because they didn't have a lot of education.

I don't think Mag loved the Texas scenery. She and Pigg took turns driving. You could never tell really what

specifically Pigg didn't like because she seldom complained. She got real enthusiastic about the things she
did like, though, and since she was quiet in the car these
days, I knew Texas wasn't one of them. Day followed day
of driving. It was hot even with the windows rolled down
and the coolness of the blue wildflowers at the side of
the road. You'd look out on those blue wildflowers, some
places wave after wave of them, and you could be a ship
out at sea. You'd think a thought like that could keep you
cool, but it can't. We were hot and cranky by day and like
Lulu and Chuck and their family by night. All through
Texas I'd erect the pup tent in the motel room at night
and go into it just to get away from Mag and Pigg. Mag
would turn up the air-conditioning full blast to drown out
even the sound of our breathing. I think if they'd been
able to fit their double beds into their pup tents they
would have used them. We still had all three in the trunk
of the car, Pigg thinking they'd use them someday again,
Mag thinking they wouldn't.

It was in Texas that we ran out of conversation completely and started to listen to Daly Kramer on the radio
every day. She came on for two hours at a time, and then
you'd find her on another channel. Sometimes we'd listen to the same broadcast repeated in the same day.
That's how bored we were. She always had good advice,
though it made you think twice about your own life and
how you were doing everything wrong. How everyone in

your family was doing everything wrong, too. There was
my dad, never home. There was my mom, going all the
way to Africa without paying attention to the rest of us.
Here I was in a car with two middle-aged aunts and no
company of my own age and no healthy baseball games
or anything, just driving aimlessly in circles around
Texas. When it got to the point I felt we were doomed, I
had to turn off the radio. When Mag and Pigg didn't want
to turn it off, I'd just put a pillow over my ears and go
back to watching the blue wildflowers. Anyhow, listening
to her radio show again and again made you look over
your shoulder at yourself all day long. I could tell it was
having the same effect on Mag and Pigg without improv-
ing any of us none. That's how we all began to talk in
Texas, like the low-class Texans we ran into in diners. At
first we did it for fun and then it kind of stuck, because
double negatives just feel so nice and smooth sliding out
the mouth. Mag and Pigg said it was a shame to have to
give it up when they went home again, and Pigg got this
strange look in her eye and said, Did we have to go
home? We should have known something was brewing
within her that very moment. But we weren't paying
close attention to each other.

We took to rehashing the day's show over dinner when
we didn't have any conversation, so now not only did we
listen to it all day long but we talked about it all night. I
was beginning to think Daly Kramer's show *caused* peo-

ple to become deeply neurotic, and I began to wonder about that man in the bookstore, the one who got his book for his birthday, how much he must have listened to her show. I mentioned this to Mag and Pigg and also that maybe doing nothing but listening to radio psychologists and talking about people's problems wasn't a very healthy life for me and maybe I should be out playing baseball with the guys, but they just looked at me with large, unseeing, bored eyes and then told me to lighten up.

"Besides," said Pigg, "you can't play baseball with the guys. The guys aren't here."

"You're in Texas now," said Mag breezily.

So then I decided that maybe things weren't as they were supposed to be but there wasn't much I could do about it in the middle of Texas. Mag was right about that. We were in Texas now. Then Mag and Pigg started discussing a woman who wanted to have her boyfriend's name tattooed on her shoulder blade and how Daly Kramer had said she was a grownup and could do whatever she liked but advised against it, so you could tell that this absolutely rained all over this woman's tattoo parade, and I got involved in that and never did bring up baseball again.

I stopped sleeping in the pup tent after a while, and before you knew it we had moved on to Oklahoma. We lost Pigg in Oklahoma.

Oklahoma

IT ALL STARTED because Pigg wanted to see what it was like to be a windmill. We had left Texas early that morning when we'd gotten a call from my mother. I was quite excited, as you might guess, and even through the crackle hiss of the phone I could make out that my father was better, his fever was down, although puzzlingly, my mother said he "would never be the same."

"What do you mean by that?" I asked.

"Are you eating properly?" asked my mother, which was a strange question because I didn't imagine I'd be eating much differently on the road. My mother never could introduce me to vegetables more exotic than the occasional tomato.

"What do you mean he won't ever be the same?"

"The phone is crackling again. What big city are you headed for? Quick, Henry, before the cell breaks up."

"Pigg, what big city are we headed for?" I asked.

"We're not headed for any big city, we're just tooling about," said Pigg.

"No, I think she wants to know . . ." I began, when I heard my mother shout to give Mag the phone, so I did. When Mag got off, she seemed a little subdued.

"I'm sorry I had to hang up, but we lost the connection," she said.

"Well, that's okay," I said, thinking it wasn't anything to get so upset about, it was always happening, after all.

"They're meeting us in Tulsa," said Mag dully.

"Who? Not Katherine and Norman?" said Pigg.

"Yes, Katherine and Norman," snapped Mag.

I had mixed feelings about this all right. I would be glad to see both of them, especially my mother because she had been lost. No, especially my father because he had been so sick. Pigg and Mag didn't look happy at the prospect of seeing either of them and I could see why. It was definitely going to cramp our style. This had been *our* little adventure.

"Well, what are we supposed to do? All just drive back together?" said Pigg.

"It's going to be awfully crowded," I said, thinking that the only thing that had made this trip at all comfortable was having the big backseat to myself. I tried to imagine myself squeezed into the middle with my mom and dad on each side of me. Then I tried to imagine, worse still, being squeezed with Mag and Pigg on each side of me. Any combination I could think of after that was too horrible for words.

"And what did she mean that my father would never be the same?" I asked.

"Oh, that was just Katherine being dramatic," said Mag. "Of course your father will be the same. He'll be exactly the same."

"Except for the malaria," said Pigg.

"Pigg, shut up," said Mag.

"Malaria recurs is what she meant," said Pigg. "Out of nowhere you get the fever and get sick all over again. Over and over and over. That's malaria for you."

"But it's no worse than a cold, right?" I said.

"Oh no," said Pigg. "No worse than that. To Africans. Now listen, Mag, how are we supposed to know when they're arriving in Tulsa?"

"She said they'd call. She's booking tickets for Tulsa and will let us know when she does."

"Don't they trust us to get Henry home?"

"Katherine does, but she said that Norman wanted a little vacation."

"A little road trip?" said Pigg.

"My father hates road trips," I said.

"Oh, look, another windmill," said Pigg. "Way off there in the distance." Pigg was always pointing out these windmills. She loved them. In the middle of nowhere you would see them standing all alone, like ships in a big empty sea. Like cathedrals. Like monuments. Spinning away in whatever wind would come along. They must have been there to power the big empty ranches we saw. You'd see ranchland, miles and miles and miles of it, cattle about and never a single soul. I guess they were out working the ranch or in their ranch houses that you never saw either. The space just sort of swallowed them up. Pigg kept pointing out the windmills until Mag looked like she was going to have a fit, but she didn't say anything. Then Pigg said, "Stop the car and let me out."

"Why?" asked Mag. "Do you want to take a picture?"

This was a strange thing to say because we hadn't taken a picture, not a single one, this whole trip. If they had a camera with them I wasn't aware of it.

"No, just drop me alongside of the road and drive until you can't see me anymore. I want to see how it feels to be like those windmills. To stand here in the middle of nothing all by myself as far as the eye can see."

"You gonna spin, too?" asked Mag, but she pulled the car to the side of the road. We really weren't doing much of anything anyway, and Mag was obviously depressed at the idea of my parents joining us soon and couldn't get it out of her immediate consciousness. I could see she was brooding something terrible.

"Just let me out," said Pigg unnecessarily because she was already climbing out of the car. "Now drive away."

So we did. We drove and drove and drove. I enjoyed watching Pigg there at the side of the road becoming smaller and smaller and farther away like she was a disappearing act until she was no more. I guess Mag was keeping track in the mirror, too, because she said, "Do you suppose we can turn around now and go back and get her?"

"Yep," I said as per Pigg's instructions.

"Serve her right if we just leave her there." Which was kind of prophetic of Mag.

We drove back, and that's when we saw a horse coming lickety-split out of nowhere with his rider hanging on something fierce. It was clearly a horse out of control, and the next second it threw the rider and took off in a cloud of dust. We sped forward as fast as we could and saw Pigg running toward the fallen rider, but there was a big fence between them. We got there as the man, who was obviously okay despite that nasty fall, climbed over the fence, which was quite a feat, as it was barbed wire, to talk to Pigg. He was the first human we'd seen all day and it was quite exciting.

We pulled up next to Pigg and the dust-covered man. Pigg opened the car door, and he climbed in the back next to me.

"Mag," said Pigg, "I said we'd give him a ride to his ranch house. That wild horse of his dumped him."

"We saw," said Mag briefly. "How do you do. I'm Magnolia and this is Henry and I guess you met Pigg."

"Pig?" said the man.

"Peg," said Pigg.

"Peg?" said Mag.

"Yes?" said Pigg, and then Mag frowned.

"My name's Cody. I own this ranch, and if you're not in a hurry, I'd be happy to show you around it. That horse you saw is a brand-new green one I'm breaking. Name of Go Lucky."

"You're lucky he didn't break your neck," said Mag. "Horses are no good. I grew up with them. No good at all."

"Wouldn't argue with you there," said Cody, and we drove along in silence after that. Pigg kept putting her hand up to brush flecks of dust out of her yellow spikes.

We drove a long way before we came to his driveway and then another long way up a dusty gravelly track to a farmhouse so small it looked like a toy replica, with a wrap-around porch and some inviting beat-up old wicker furniture on it. He invited us to plop ourselves in those dusty old chairs and went inside for a big pitcher of iced tea, which tasted pretty fine right about then.

"Do I look okay?" Pigg whispered to Mag, trying to catch her reflection in the window and wiping her cheeks down in case there was road dust on them.

Mag just sighed and looked out toward the barn, where various horses were hanging out.

"So," said Cody as we settled down with our iced tea. A curious awkwardness came upon the porch, not like there generally is when strangers are just being friendly and you're hanging out for a suspended moment in time before you go your separate ways. This was different. "Where you folks from?"

"Virginia," said Pigg, not saying Critz or Floyd.

"Never been," said Cody. "Never been most places."

Then he dropped his drink on the table and ran out into the yard because Go Lucky had just come galloping back and he was going to have a little tussle with him right there and show him who was boss. It looked to me like Cody was behaving like a maniac, but Mag said you always had to do that with horses, be dominant or they ruled you completely, and no one wanted to be ruled by a 1,200-pound animal.

"Mental control," chanted Pigg and Mag together, putting their fingers to their temples in an obviously time-honored family visual aid.

"You don't ever want to be dominated by anything, but particularly not a horse," said Mag.

I must say Cody was a cowboy right down to the boots and the name. He looked like what you'd pick from central casting if they said give me a cowboy, except that he was so short. He was no taller than Pigg, but he was all muscle and bone in a wiry mesh of a man. He was fast with that horse, putting on a new saddle, which the horse kept trying to buck off, and then getting on him and staying on him despite the horse's protesting and bucking around. When the horse had quieted down, he got off again and untacked and put him away and then he came back to us.

"Stupid horse lost the saddle out there somewhere. I better ride out and find it," he said. "You all want to come? I got enough horses for all of us."

Well, I wanted to come and so did Pigg. Mag said she thought she'd just sit on the porch and enjoy some iced tea, so Cody told her to make herself at home and went off to saddle up a gentle old horse for me and a pretty good horse for Pigg, who said she could ride not too bad. "I don't look like I was raised in any fancy riding school or anything," said Pigg, "but I won't embarrass you by falling off either."

"I don't embarrass so easy," said Cody, and helped her up, though it didn't look to me like she needed it. I was the one who needed it. I'd never been up on a horse before, and once I was I didn't see what all the fuss was about. Far as I could see, you just sat there in that big hollowed-out saddle and kept your feet in the stirrups and your horse followed the other horses. When I said this, both Cody and Pigg laughed, but I didn't see why, seemed a reasonable observation to me, it was more as if they wanted to hear the sound of themselves laughing at the same thing.

We rode for quite a long time and I was beginning to see why cowboys wore hats. I felt all sunburnt and dirty and dry, and Pigg and I were squinting in the bright light. We finally found the cast-off saddle and Cody leaped down and hauled it back up on his horse with him and then we rode home. The countryside wasn't beautiful like the lush green hills of Virginia, but it had a certain scrubby charm. Kind of understated, which I generally go for anyway. You don't want things that shout out their beauty in a braggy way. You kind of like to discover it for yourself so you feel like a part of it.

When we got back, some woman was talking to Mag and they were going at it hammer and tongs in an animated way that Mag certainly had not been with Cody.

"Ah, that's my sister, Liesl," said Cody, getting down to put our horses away. Pigg said she'd help him, so the two of them trotted off to the barn, and I went to get another very welcome drink and meet Liesl, who had invited us for supper. Mag had told her the whole story and said we'd go find a motel room and then come back after we'd washed up, if that was okay, but Liesl said we should forget finding a motel room, there wasn't anything for miles and miles, at least sixty or seventy, she estimated. We should stay right there in the house and she and Cody would take the bunkhouse. She said they kept it for when they hired help, which they did summers oftentimes, but right now it was empty. She wouldn't put us up there, she said. It really wasn't fit for ladies and children. The ranch hands wrote nasties on the walls when they got bored.

Mag said we couldn't take her house, and Liesl said, Oh, sure you can, Cody wouldn't have it any other way, and they were bored with only each other to talk to night and day. We'd be a real treat, some conversation at dinner. They'd gotten to the point where mostly they just grunted at each other. I could understand that, that was the way we were in Texas—that was Texas all over. Mag said she didn't know, and I didn't blame her, it was a bit weird staying at someone's house like that who you didn't know, just out of the blue. When Cody and Pigg got back, Pigg accepted the invitation with wild enthusiasm but Mag said, Pigg, didn't we have to get on to Tulsa?

"Did you call her Pig?" asked Liesl through the kitchen window that looked out to the porch. She was inside chopping vegetables for dinner.

"PEG!" called Pigg.

"Oh, PEG, *of course*," said Liesl. "It just sounded like Pig."

"Well, that's a Virginia accent for you," said Pigg.

We ended up eating dinner and staying there. Liesl changed the sheets and made the two upstairs bedrooms cozy, doing stuff that was by and large unnecessary, like putting little rosette-type soaps in the bathroom that you were afraid to use, which I wouldn't anyway, not wishing to smell roselike myself, but it seemed to make her happy, which our presence did generally, which was gratifying as I really wasn't doing anything but being there. I don't know what it did for Mag or Pigg. Pigg seemed pretty much in heaven anyway, and I'm guessing if it wasn't for this what you might call hyperhospitableness, Mag would have been completely unbearable. She was acting as if she had sand in her underwear as it was.

I got Cody's room and Pigg and Mag were sleeping in Liesl's room, one on the double bed and one on her chaise longue that was set up by a window from which you could see the whole ranch and the sunset and night sky of stars. It was one of those slanted-ceilinged bedrooms, big and bright, with thin curtains fluttering in the breeze. It felt like the ranch, full of space and light and a place where a person could feel like there wasn't anything but good things in the world. I personally wished I could sleep there and look out at that sunset over the big land and see those stars flashing in the dark sky all night, but it had been a long day and I was thankful to have any bed by the time I climbed into it. Cody's bed wasn't by the window, so I was just sitting at the window, looking out, before making my way to the bed, half falling asleep on the sill, when I heard Mag's furious whisper floating through their open window: "You're falling in love with that man, now don't deny it, Pigg."

"Peg," said Pigg.

We were there three more days before my parents called to tell us when they'd be in Tulsa. I almost forgot what we were doing there at all. I think Mag would have preferred to be tooling about Oklahoma, bedding down in Tulsa or almost anything else, but we couldn't have left Liesl, she looked about ready to cry any time anyone brought it up. Finally, when my parents called, they said they'd be in Tulsa in two days' time and we were but two days' driving from Tulsa anyhow, so Mag said with evident relief, "Well, that's it! Time's up! Time to go!" It was just me and her and Liesl on the porch because Pigg was off riding with Cody again. She said she was helping him, and that always made Mag gag. I got to talk to my dad for the first time in what seemed an awfully long while. He sounded kind of weak and sick, but when he heard we were on a ranch he offered his usual good advice. "Don't get up on any of those horses, boy," he said. "Remember it's just as easy to fall off a horse as it is to get on one." Well, I didn't think it was so easy to get on one myself. I'd finally stopped needing help getting up, but I wouldn't have objected to it.

Anyhow, I'd pretty much stopped riding along with Pigg and Cody because I wasn't so stupid I didn't know when I wasn't wanted, and I sure wasn't wanted there, not when they had sixty miles of ranchland and a lot of unsuspecting cattle to be alone with. That was as private a way to conduct a romance as I could think of. My father seemed relieved when I told him I wasn't riding anymore and that I'd see him in Tulsa in one piece.

"Well, that makes one of us," he said mysteriously, and hung up.

When Cody and Pigg finally came back for dinner, and while Liesl, who I swear looked about ready to hang herself Western-style from the nearest tree, was busy putting dinner on the table, Mag dropped the bomb about how we had to leave the next morning for Tulsa. I was surprised when Pigg and Cody didn't say much about this, just "Um" and "Oh yeah?" in a way that you might think downright cold and matter-of-fact if you didn't know what was about to happen next, which we did not, although Mag seemed relieved and not to notice their odd response. Enough nonsense, I could tell from the slope of her shoulders, was what she was thinking.

It wasn't until the next morning, when we were actually standing on the porch, that Pigg said to Mag, "I'm not going."

Well, that was a shocker. "You're not going where, Pigg?" asked Mag.

"I'm not going to Tulsa," said Pigg.

"What do you mean you aren't going to Tulsa?" asked Mag.

This was becoming monotonous and I wished they'd just get to the meat and clear all this up.

"I'm not going any further with you."

"Well, excuse me, Pigg, but just what *are* you going to do?"

"I'm staying here. On the ranch," said Pigg defiantly. "Cody has asked me to stay on and I said yes. And I'm going to marry him, too, Mag."

"You're WHAT?" said Mag. "You've known him, what, three days?"

"I can't help that. I could know him all my life, wouldn't make a difference. That's what I'm doing. There's no use trying to talk me out of it. None at all. I'll *give* you my half of the business for deserting you like this, Mag, and someday I'll come get my stuff, but in the meantime do you think you could send me some stuff if I made a list? Gosh, I'll need clothes and . . ." Pigg looked dreamily into the air as if taking inventory already.

Well, Mag didn't know what to say to this. I reminded Pigg of how much she respected Daly Kramer and how many times Daly Kramer had advised people to know someone at least a *year* before marrying. I just didn't think Daly Kramer would approve of this at all. Folly, folly. But Pigg said she wasn't interested in what Daly Kramer had to say. That all the sensible rules for following just didn't make a lick of sense when you met someone like Cody. She couldn't care less for Daly Kramer and her way to make things work out. But thanks anyway, she said, patting my shoulder, because I guess she thought she'd been a mite emphatic.

Well, Mag got into the car like one struck dumb, which I guess she was because we didn't say much for oh, about two hundred miles, I guess it was. We drove so much that sometimes I thought we must be driving in circles; I'm sure there couldn't be all that much to Oklahoma as we were seeing, and finally we stopped for a cold iced tea and Mag turned to me in the seat next to her and said, "Can you beat that?"

"If that don't beat all," I agreed, happy to put my tongue to use again.

"Well, I guess it's just you and me," said Mag. "I don't guess it's going to work out."

And she called Pigg that night from the motel to see if she'd changed her mind. She called her every night thereafter, every single night forever, but Pigg never did change her mind, only her name, which she did legally and without ever telling Cody it was really Pigg. She became Peg forever after that, and I say it's a good thing.

So that's how Mag and I ended up driving alone to Tulsa, and I'll tell you this, at first, in our shell-shocked state, it wasn't so bad. At least we knew Pigg was happy. But as we set out the next day for the Tulsa airport, on a long lone stretch of highway where all we saw in terms of living things was a couple of hawks circling long slow lazy circles, and I thought we were both just riding along thinking our own lazy thoughts in circles like the hawks, Mag reached over and picked up Daly Kramer's book from the floor of the front seat where she and Pigg had kept it, reading bits to each other, and she flung it out the window without a word.

Colorado

THINGS WERE MOSTLY SILENT the rest of the way to the Tulsa airport. It became awkward, just me and Mag in the car. Before, I could sort of rest my brain, Mag and Pigg were so comfortable with each other and we were all so comfortable with me being part of the upholstery, there wasn't any self-consciousness involved, but now with Pigg gone, I guess Mag and I thought we had to find some conversation between the two of us and that made for an awfully heavy silence in the car, not to mention she was still so mad. I think she was a bit poleaxed, too, like thinking, What am I going to do with the whole business and the whole house to myself? Maybe she was so used to it being her and Pigg she didn't know what it would be like just her, like they were two puzzle pieces fit together or one of those Russian dolls with all the other dolls inside it, only now it was an empty doll. Or maybe not. Maybe she was just tired of doing all the driving herself.

At the airport my parents' plane was late. It seemed to me you always had to wait for the things you were most anxious for. So Mag took me to a bookstore right there in the airport and got me a book. It didn't look like a very good book, but there wasn't much to choose from. I was surprised to find a bookstore at all. I'd never been in an airport. But there were all kinds of stores and restaurants and fuss. I kept watching people coming and going and thinking that they were bringing us germs from all parts of the world, but maybe that's just because I was so aware my father was coming back with malaria. I know Mag said he wasn't contagious, but I think you never can tell about these things. Africa's a big country, and seems to me there might be different, more dangerous kinds of malaria than Mag and Pigg knew about. I read quietly in a chair and tried not to touch much. I don't want to sound too fastidious because I'm not—let's face it, I'd been using gas station bathrooms for weeks—but it did seem to me that airports had potential to be one of the dirtiest places on Earth and I'd already had enough dirt this trip to last me a lifetime.

Mag had bought herself a magazine, but she didn't sit and read it, she was too busy pacing about, jumping in and out of the chair next to me, getting herself cups of coffee, watching the planes go up and down or at least staring in their direction; she had piercing, unseeing eyes that day like there was an awful lot going on behind them that I'd never know about. Especially since I made the comment about the hair. On one of Mag's little rests in the seat next to me between her nervous twitching forays, I turned to her and said as it just occurred to me, "Good thing she got that haircut."

"What?" said Mag, looking through me with those weird eyes she'd had since leaving Pigg.

"Pigg's haircut," I said slowly, pronouncing each syllable as if speaking to the hearing-impaired. "Her blond spikes that she did to look younger. Good thing she got it before meeting up with this fellow. She kind of made herself attractive just in the nick of time."

Mag's mouth opened and closed, opened and closed like a fish, and then she got up and rushed off without saying anything at all and after that she came back and said, "Are you implying that I'm not attractive?"

"What do you mean?" I said in honest astonishment. "I wasn't talking about you at all. I was talking about Pigg. Pigg and her haircut!"

"But you're implying, aren't you, that I don't tend to my natural beauty?"

"Well, it seems to me if it's so natural, you don't *need* to tend to it," I said. I could tell immediately this was the wrong thing to say. It was like pouring gasoline on a grass fire.

"I see. I see. So Pigg is the good-looking one and I am the troll?"

"I didn't say that," I said.

"You didn't have to," said Mag.

"Yeah, I didn't have to and I didn't," I said in a small voice because Mag was already storming off to the bathroom. I wondered if she was going in there to brush her hair. It did look a mess, truth to tell. But when she came out she didn't speak to me, and she didn't speak to me for a whole twenty-four hours after that. Could be we'd just had about enough of each other, confined as we'd been in the car. Funny how much smaller that car seemed when there was one person less in it.

Finally, when I was about ready to give up, my parents' plane came in and they walked through the gate door looking a little uncertain and shell-shocked, but they focused as soon as they saw me. My father gave me a big hug first and then my mother, who whispered, "Don't worry about a thing," in my ear, which prompted me to immediately start worrying.

Because their plane was late, it was real dark out, we were tired, and they looked about dead, we did something we hadn't done on this trip, which was to stay the night in a city. There was a big Holiday Inn right by the airport, and that's where we pulled up. My dad and Mag went in to get rooms. They got a room for Mag and a room for my mother and a room for my father, and then my parents asked me which room did I want to stay in and I thought, Uh-oh, this cannot be good.

We lit out the next morning for Colorado, and if I thought my place in the car had changed, it *really* changed after my parents joined us. I was used to invalids sprawling in the car, so my father slumped or riding with the front passenger seat reclining was nothing new to me, and the awkwardness I had with Mag was over now that we had my parents as buffers, so to speak, but I'd lost the feeling temporarily that anything could happen to me because it couldn't, my parents were protecting me from *that*, and it gave me a kind of smothery feeling after the freedom of the road and my aunts' lackadaisical care. My mother, for instance, was concerned about my homework being done on some kind of a schedule, which I'd already given up as a completely ridiculous notion and Pigg and Mag hadn't paid attention to from day one. So my long fruitful days of staring out the window whenever I pleased were interrupted and put in serious jeopardy by my mom's need for order in the car and I got math crammed down my throat at what I thought were scenic and inappropriate times.

Mostly my father slept. My mom and Mag did the driving and talked a good deal between the two of them. We were driving to Colorado because Mag had wanted to get at least that far across the country. She kept emphasizing *at least*, leaving my parents no wiggle room, never mind that they had just been in the wilds of Africa catching diseases. Mag wasn't ready to go home and one sister had already pretty much ruined the trip; she wasn't letting another one.

"You can take Henry and fly on home alone, or rent a car and go without me back to Virginia, but I'm going to Mesa Verde," said Mag.

"What is so special about Mesa Verde?" asked my mother. "Haven't you seen enough? I think Norman needs to go home."

"Then *take* him home," said Mag. "I don't know how you know what Norman wants anyway, you haven't spoken two words to him since you got out of the airplane."

We thought my father was sleeping, but at this he opened his eyes and said, "All I want, Katherine, is for you to never speak to me again."

"Oh, you do not, Norman," said my mother, but she looked worried. "It's not my fault you got malaria."

"I don't want to rehash this," said my father. "I want to sleep." And closed his eyes and refused to say anything else even though it was clear he was awake. It was giving me a stomach knot, but fortunately it didn't bother Mag, who was busily arguing with my mother about Mesa Verde and saying that as far as she was concerned she didn't have to account for anything to either of my parents, but if they must know, over the years, she and Pigg had made a list of all the places they planned to go some-day if they ever had time to see the world.

"And Mesa Verde was on the list," said Mag stubbornly.

I knew that tone of voice of Mag's and knew that we'd be going to Mesa Verde, and we did. My father was really much too tired and floppy to argue about anything. He was kind of like taking a big bag of sand along. You just flung him around from place to place. I wondered hopefully at first if that's why my parents were staying in separate rooms, but it wasn't. The only reason they were in separate rooms was because they wanted to be. I alternated staying the night with each of them, and my mom refused to talk about my dad, but my dad, when he spoke about my mom, said that he had given up on her. In Africa, something in him had broken. And he was simply furious with Pigg and Mag for losing me in Florida even though I kept telling him that I had been fine. They hadn't lost me so much as I'd gone on down the creek and then things just happened. But my dad wanted to assign blame, and blame had been assigned. I had been willing to assign the blame to Mag and Pigg, too, when I could use it to manipulate some goodies, but it seemed pointless when he did it and all he got out of it was an uncomfortable silence.

We stopped for the night in a motel outside Durango.

Colorado

There were a lot of fake cowboys in Durango; after meeting Cody I was pretty good at telling the difference. A
man with no muscle or color who's got time to go shopping midday in boutiques is not a cowboy for all that he's
got the right hat and boots. Durango had so many fake
cowboys they could have rounded up all the longhorns in
Texas and had enough hands for a cattle drive if any of
them'd had time for it, which they probably didn't, being
too busy on their cell phones making deals. I would have
aired all these observations in a car with Pigg and Mag
and we would've had a good go of it, arguing the matter
back and forth, but I wasn't introducing any ideas to my
parents in the atmosphere of that car, which was strictly a
no-talk zone.

One of the things my father had mentioned to me the
night before—it was my turn to sleep in his hotel room—
was how seriously flawed my mother was. How she'd always been seriously flawed but he'd somehow managed
to overlook it the first twenty years of their marriage or
something. How she always did exactly what she wanted
with no regard for anyone else. This made me a bit un-
easy as it was just the way Chet had talked about her, but
I couldn't understand how you could know her and put
that kind of spin on her actions. It wasn't that she did just
what she wanted, it was more as if she didn't think about
how she affected people because she knew we were all
okay every minute even if we didn't know that. And I

knew that my mother was angry with my father because he blamed her for things but that my father just wanted so desperately for everything to turn out okay and he saw her as continually throwing obstacles in his path. It made me sad that I couldn't get either one of them to see each other the way I saw them. I was sure if I could that they would stop all this unpleasantness and we'd have some peace. Then, the next morning, he said, quite dramatically, that sometimes something could break inside you and that would be it for you and that person. "Your mother has just done things that are inexplicable on my moral compass."

"Well, if it's a choice between Mom and a moral compass, I choose Mom!" I said, and stormed right out of his motel room and ran into Mag, who was having a cigarette.

"Mag!" I said, shocked.

"There's nothing I hate more than some little snot-nosed kid telling a grownup in a sanctimonious voice, when they've never experienced the world properly, how they shouldn't be doing these unhealthy things that are maybe saving their sanity," said Mag. And then she lit another right off the first, which I'm sure she wouldn't have done had I not been there to witness it, so, in a way, you could say I was exacerbating the habit.

"I don't give a small rat's poop if you smoke," I said, which was the rudest thing I'd said on this trip, but I was up to my ears with my parents' opinions of each other and had planned on dumping it on Mag, but now I could see that wasn't going to happen, so I just stormed back to my room, got packed up, and went to wait in the car while the grownups had breakfast. My mother brought me a muffin, but I just held it stonily in my hand all the way to Mesa Verde, and on those windy cliffside roads I opened my window and tossed it down, down, down into the great abyss of the American countryside, defiling all that rich pure wilderness with my stupid little muffin. I can't say it made me feel any better, but it didn't make me feel any worse.

It was late in the day and hot and we were at a low point energy-wise by the time the car started snaking up the long spiraling drive to Mesa Verde. The visitors' center looked to be about at the top where the cave dwellings were, and we stopped there for a minute, but my parents thought it was boring; turned out that they didn't like visitors' centers as much as Pigg and Mag and I did. We kind of liked any place where you could get free color brochures and baseball caps and a nice overflowing ice cream. This visitors' center was no different and offered slide shows and a place to buy tickets to go on a tour of the cave dwellings.

"I've never been much of one for tours," said my mother.

"Well, you certainly proved that in Africa," said my father.

"Norman . . ." said my mother.

"Can we just go see the caves?" said Mag in a long-suffering tone.

Well, it turned out to take forever to get up there because the road snaked around hairpin turns, nothing between us and several thousand feet of open space going straight down. I clung to the seat as if that would keep the car on the road, and Mag made me crazy by driving with one foot on the accelerator and the other propped up on the seat so that she rode with one knee bent in front of the steering wheel. It was an unlawfully casual way to drive to begin with, but it was way too casual for those roads and she was taking the turns at fifty miles an hour when the speed limit sign said clearly to go at thirty. I would have been tempted to say something, but I didn't have to because my mother and father were both nagging her at that point.

"You're going way too fast," said my mother. "Look at the speed limit."

"Oh, for heaven's sakes," said Mag. "Nobody follows the speed limit. Nobody goes thirty miles an hour."

"That's what it's *there* for, because that's the safe speed. Slow down."

"And take your foot off the seat," my father joined in.

"You shut up, you've done nothing but lie there all day," said Mag.

"The man has MALARIA," said my mother.

"And how did I *get* malaria?" asked my father.

And on and on and on. I would have put on Pigg's discarded radio earphones, but I was too scared. It's not that
I was anxious to hear everyone's screams as we went over
the edge, but all your animal instincts tell you to keep
eyes and ears aware in such situations, so I had to listen to
everything everyone hated about everyone else all the
way up the mountain. When we finally got to the top, it
turned out the only way you could see the caves was to be
on a tour; they didn't let you just go down alone and have
a look around. We were an hour away from the visitors'
center where the tickets were sold. Going back for tickets
meant not just two more hours of driving but driving
those terrifying curves again, and it was already three
o'clock. The last tour went out at four. It was moot.

Mag was in a white-hot fury, I could tell. But she
didn't say anything. Instead we decided to hike around on
the trails at the top in the blazing shadeless sun and look
at the people in the cool caves, being intelligently informed about things we could only guess at.

"Are you mad at me for not getting us tour tickets?" my
mom asked Mag as we wiped sweat off our brows and realized we should also have gotten some water. We were
an hour from that, too.

"We came all the way to Mesa Verde and we're not going to see the caves because you don't like tours," Mag
said.

I could feel it coming, the fighting, the recriminations. I began to pace faster and faster in a small circle of dust I was creating.

"Do you have to yell?" asked my father. He was sweating and leaning against a rock and looking like death. "I do believe you ladies are going to finish me off. You and your little adventures. Start the process in Africa and go in for the kill in Colorado."

I ran my hands through my hair as I paced. My hair was soaked with sweat and the dust created a kind of mud, which caused it to stick on end.

"Oh, stop whining," said Mag.

"I was never lost in Africa! You never had to worry. Mag, please leave Norman alone!" said my mother.

"I don't need you to stick up for me," said my father. "Does anyone CARE that I had MALARIA?"

I looked down at the caves, at all those placid people listening with calm, utilizing this educational opportunity, nobody screaming at their family members. I ran my sweat-and-dirt-covered hands over my face as I watched my own family fighting at a natural wonder.

"Oh, please, could we not hear about malaria for ten minutes?" said Mag. "Katherine, you're always doing things to drive everyone crazy."

"The man has had MALARIA!" said my mother as if that explained everything.

That's when I stopped pacing and stomped my foot

into that stony ground as hard as I could. I tilted my head up into the great open sky and yelled, "HOW DID I END UP WITH ALL YOU UNPLEASANT PEOPLE?" And for a second it seemed to reverberate into a great silence while they took me in. It did seem as if every last person I loved was simply unbearably unpleasant and that I really should have been born into a nicer family. But I don't think this occurred to them. They just looked at me as if I'd, puzzlingly, for no good reason, gone nuts.

"Henry, hush," said my mother, while Mag and my dad said similar "Cut that out," and "Keep your voice down" things, and then we decided to get back in the car and go get a Coke and a hot dog, which they clearly thought would restore my good spirits, and, sadly, it did.

Then we drove on down the last of the winding roads. When we got to the bottom of the mountain, Mag said, "Next stop Mount Rushmore."

Mount Rushmore

THERE WAS A WHOLE LOT OF COUNTRY between Mount Rushmore and Mesa Verde. We backtracked through Colorado and over its mountains. If you like mountains, it was swell. My mother, it turned out, loved them and kept uttering little shrieks of glee and pointing out how this or that looked like Africa until my father told her politely to shut up. He was getting better, you could tell: he didn't look so inert but had a bit of life to him, which was a pleasant change. I'd seen two people now on this trip convalesce and come back to health in the car, and it made me wonder about the restorative power of road food.

Then we got to Deadwood and I got sick. It's a wonder really it hadn't happened to me or Mag or Pigg before. But after all those germy gas station bathrooms, you'd kind of think you'd be dead by now. Dead in Deadwood,

I thought to myself in despair as I lay around the motel room, throwing up. My parents and Mag were going to take turns caring for me, but I really preferred my mother because I was more used to her care. If you wanted actual hands-on care you went to my mother; if you wanted little maxims about life, you went to my dad. However, I was touched by how all three of them came and went, bringing me books and ginger ale and tempting little treats like plain toast without anything, not even jam. "I don't think I can get better on plain toast," I said to Mag because it was her turn to be solicitous, so she went out and got me a cheeseburger, which seemed a good idea at the time until I threw it up all over her. "I'm really sorry, Mag," I said.

"From now on you're getting toast," she said, and I could see her point. My mother was the only person who could ever stand to have me throw up on her. I threw up on everyone that weekend, and my father didn't seem any more crazy about it than Mag, although he was stoic.

"Don't worry, boy," he said. "We all throw up on someone now and then. Try to aim for the wastebasket, is all. Try to anticipate and aim."

I promised him I would, but you can't always. You don't always see it coming.

On Monday I was the one recovering in the car and we started out again for Mount Rushmore. By then my parents were getting along a bit better. They hadn't forgiven each other or anything, not that my mother ever seemed mad exactly, more like she was making herself a stone so she couldn't absorb any of my father's anger. They kept a polite distance from each other, but I considered that a start.

Over eggs at a restaurant on the way to Devils Tower, which my dad wanted to see and Mag allowed—I think she was just glad that someone else was getting into the trip—we discovered that my mother loved souvenirs. I think *she* discovered that she loved souvenirs. They had all kinds of Devils Tower souvenirs at this restaurant: pictures of the rock, statues of the rock, make-your-own-rock kits. She bought fourteen postcards and a fridge magnet. When we got to Devils Tower she said, "Now, this *really* looks like Africa," and my father didn't say a thing. It was possible, I thought, that he couldn't quite understand how she could be so nostalgic for a country that had given him malaria, but I understood. After all, it was my mother's one big adventure.

When we got to Mount Rushmore we spent a lot of time in the cafeteria, where you can sit by these huge picture windows and look at the monument. It was a pretty amazing thing, all those faces in the rocks, made by dynamite, no less. Pretty spectacular engineering feat, as my father said. My mother bought an impossible amount of postcards and another fridge magnet and a T-shirt for me that said "Mount Rushmore," which I must say I didn't really want. Neither Mag nor Pigg nor I had bought anything on this trip, unless you count books. It was too much like trying to take some part of the trip with you, and as excited as I had been getting to places on this trip, I found it was just as satisfying to leave them behind.

Mag and my mom and I sat at a table and ate Danishes while my dad went to see an educational film about Mount Rushmore.

"I'm not much of one for educational films," said my mother. And neither Mag nor my father said anything sarcastic about tours or monkeys in Africa or anything, so I breathed easy. Things were beginning to ease up for sure, I decided. When my dad came back, we all sat and looked at Mount Rushmore some more, and my dad took me for a little walk on a windy terrace so we could see it from different angles and he could tell me the gist of it, the details, as usual with the two of us, being lost completely. "And the man who made it died right before the final blasting, so he never saw it completed," said my father.

"Gosh, that was bad luck," I said.

"So it just goes to show," he said, "you gotta use the time you have coming to you, boy."

I nodded, but even I didn't really see what this had to do with the poor man who died making this great thing and I don't think he did either. I could tell he just felt a need to conclude, and it began to become apparent to me on this trip that this need to conclude after events might do more harm than good in terms of seeing things as they actually were. But it did give you a pleasant feeling of order in the universe, so you knew where you were. And sometimes my dad's conclusions made me feel nice and secure, even when they made no sense. Then it turned out that there was only so long you could look at the monument. My parents went to find restrooms and Mag and I stood out on the windy terrace looking at Mount Rushmore from yet more angles.

"There's only so long you can look at anything," I said to Mag. "I'm ready to go back to the car." I didn't want to disappoint my parents by telling them this. That had been one of the good things about going with Mag and Pigg: they didn't care that much about everything being so special and wonderful and perfect for me. To tell you the truth, if I'd walked off the edge of Mesa Verde, they would probably have looked down and said, Well, that was unfortunate, and continued their trip. So I was free to move around in my own skin, and it turned out I liked my own skin fine. I never had to worry about worrying them by not everything always *being* so special and wonderful and perfect. I could just say, Let's get the heck out of here, when the spirit moved me. It was a whole lot easier way to live and it didn't give you a twist in your stomach all the time.

"I don't know what I'm supposed to be thinking about

it, is all," I said as Mag and I continued to look at Mount Rushmore.

"It's the beach all over again," said Mag.

My parents came back and we drove through the Badlands National Park then, and that was enjoyable. It was real desolate and you could look at and pass through it and it wasn't any big deal like Mount Rushmore was supposed to be, so I enjoyed it a whole lot more, and when we left it behind I didn't feel like I had to conclude anything.

"I thought you'd want to stay at a motel by Mount Rushmore," said my mother when it was her turn to sit up front with Mag as Mag drove. "You traveled all this way to see it."

"You don't know anything about anything, do you?" said Mag, which was kind of raw, but my mom just filed her nails and looked contentedly at the passing landscape.

"Can I stick my feet out the window?" I asked Mag because sometimes they got awfully hot in that car. I don't know why my feet got hot; no one else's seemed to.

Mag looked up and down the highway and nodded. There wasn't another car in sight, nothing for miles but the wind bending the lone low grasslands, its arrival visible a long time before you felt it. I rolled down the window and stuck my bare feet out to the breeze, wiggling my toes, and my feet were awfully happy all the way to Kansas. It was in Kansas that my dad killed the cat.

Cat-Squishing Day

KANSAS IS AN AWFULLY NICE STATE and the folks that live there were awfully nice. You could tell just by the way they behaved at the motor court, nodding hello to each other and tipping their baseball caps. Most of the people in Kansas at the motor court were already from Kansas. That seemed an extraordinary thing to me. What did they do? Just go around from place to place in Kansas? We went out for dinner in a swell restaurant where they brought you thick steaks and big fluffy rolls and the waitress was genuinely happy to see you. "This has it all over Virginia Beach," I said to Mag. We had stopped in a mall that afternoon to get me more reading material, and Mag had picked out a book about artichokes. "I don't see how she's going to grow them in Oklahoma," said Mag. "The climate's all wrong." She and Pigg spoke every night, and Pigg had told her happily about her plan to grow artichokes on ten acres that Cody was giving her for that purpose, because she had suddenly gotten interested in them. "Cody is very supportive," said Pigg.

After that, Mag's conversation was all centered on artichokes and got awfully dull for the rest of us. I guess it was what you'd call an obsession. She was obsessed for Pigg's sake. It was quite touching in a tragic, desperate way.

My father ate his first full meal in that steak restaurant. Up until then he had been picking at his food, but in Kansas he ate an entire steak and many of the fluffy rolls that the waitress kept bringing with such abandon and no regard for how it would affect the overhead.

The next morning when he got up, my father said, "I think I can drive today."

"Well, I don't know, Norman," said Mag. "Better give it a few days. You look pretty peaked still."

It was true. My father might be eating like a farmhand again, but he looked about to blow over in a good breeze. Not that I think this was Mag's concern. She just wanted to keep him at passenger-seat status.

"I'm driving," said my father, and that was that.

My mother sat nervously in the backseat with me, reaching out and clutching my knee in terror from time to time when my father took the speed up to sixty. We were on country backroads because country backroads were one of the things Pigg had added to the list and Mag was honoring not only the artichoke enterprise but Pigg's unfulfilled wishes.

"I sure hope that cowboy takes her someplace sometime," said Mag.

"I'm sure he will," said my mother, dabbing at her eyes. My mother got all choked up whenever she thought about weddings. She was a definite weeper. Birthdays, anniversaries, people's scrapbooks—even scrapbooks of people she didn't know that well—parades, Fourth of July picnics. The only thing that didn't make her cry was the poor old men and women at the Mustard Seed where she worked with the homeless. It just made her set her mouth tightly. Which made me think that crying, for her, was more of a recreational activity.

Kansas was so nice that you wouldn't think someone would find fault with it, but my dad didn't like the mockingbirds. We heard them in our motor court rooms and down country roads and even at the drive-throughs.

"Oh, stop complaining about the mockingbirds," my mother said in despair at one point, putting her hand up to her forehead and wiping off a bunch of sweat. It didn't help that it was getting hotter and hotter as we moved into summer. The car was hot. We were hot. The Midwest was hot.

"I guess you'd rather me complain about having malaria."

And they were off. I couldn't understand why my father

wouldn't just forgive my mother. After dinner the night of the mockingbird complaint I took a little walk with him. Sometimes, not often, but sometimes my father liked to smoke a cigar, so we were walking downtown, close enough to the motel to walk back to it but still among the old brick false-front stores, looking for a tobacco store. We finally found one, not just a newsstand but a real cigar store, which pleased my father, and he spent a long time choosing just the one he wanted; then he lit it.

"Dad, I don't think Mom meant for you to get malaria," I said.

"You make it worse, you always have, her being the way she is," said my father. I couldn't believe now he was blaming me. I began to think maybe malaria had addled his brain as well.

"How do I make it worse?" I asked, shrinking into the sidewalk. My father rarely found fault with me.

"Your mother thinks all she has to do is hide behind motherhood and you and she can do whatever she likes. You love her no matter what, and that just makes her own natural tendency for selfishness worse."

"But how can you say she is selfish?" I asked. "I don't even know why you see her that way. Or Chet either."

"What do you know about your grandfather?" asked my father.

"We stopped and saw him," I said. "On the way through Kentucky and Tennessee."

"What did he say about your mother?"

"He didn't like her," I said, "He said she never did any of the things she was supposed to."

"Well, he was right," said my father.

That night it was my turn to stay in my mom's room, so I asked her if she still loved my dad and she said, "Your father's acting like a complete jerk," and refused to talk about it anymore and I decided that this wasn't a definite no, so there was hope.

My father continued to do a lot of the driving. I think he liked it because he could grip the wheel and glare at the road and have important things to do without having to talk to anyone. My mom and Mag mostly sipped sweating bottles of iced tea we got from convenience stores, shopping whenever their bottles began to run low. They fanned themselves and swung their crossed legs, murmuring, "My, oh my. My, oh *my*, it's *hot*," as if any of us hadn't noticed. I wasn't feeling so pert. My father and mother were not speaking at all to each other now, as if my little talks pulling forth their true feelings had made them gel into something more solid and horrible than they would have without my help.

Oh good, Henry, I thought, nice job. Mag had stopped trying to talk to them and become all interested in wedding things now and bought bride magazines and, when we stayed by small towns, would go into bridal finery stores and poke around in the bridesmaid dresses and call

Pigg to tell her what she'd found. She thought Pigg was pretty lucky to be able to vet bridal finery all across the United States, thanks to her. Then one night my mom and I heard Mag shouting in her room and my mom went and knocked on the door. I would have let Mag alone, myself, but my mom dragged me in.

"What was *that* all about?" asked my mom as Mag stood in the center of the room with the cell phone in her hand and a wild look in her eyes.

"Who do you think is going to be Pigg's maid of honor?" asked Mag.

"Well, I thought it would be you," said my mother. "But obviously not."

"Liesl?" I guessed because they did seem to get along and I could see Pigg might choose her to make Cody happy or even to make Liesl happy, figuring Mag would understand.

"Try again," said Mag.

We gave up.

"Go Lucky!" said Mag.

"The horse?" I said.

"The horse!" said Mag. "Well, I may as well stop looking for bridesmaid dresses. I hope she appreciates that."

"I couldn't be the maid of honor anyway," said my mother reflectively. "Because I'm married. I'd have to be the matron of honor."

"I suppose I'll have to start looking in tack stores now for bridal tack!" said Mag, indignantly.

I could see that Mag had a new obsession besides artichokes. She was going to be busy. We all went downtown to look for tack stores. Then we went out for ice cream. We went out for ice cream a lot because my mom had missed it in Africa.

Kansas was a whole lot of farms. Farms and farms, and you'd see men on tractors and they looked all sweaty and sunburnt and thick like they ate their wives' heavy mac-and-cheese casseroles and maybe half a pig at night, and I'd think of their happy home lives, probably going to football games and chaperoning high school dances and going to church and everyone saying grace around the table and all being worried about the same things at the same time.

We drove down a nice country road where we were going kind of slow because there was a fruit stand coming up that my mom wanted my dad to stop at and they were arguing about that and my dad was getting more and more hot under the collar, saying he'd been driving all day and he didn't want to stop at any gosh-darned fruit stand that was covered in flies, and my mother said she fancied one of their apples and my father said it was summer, the apples would be from last fall anyhow, and my mother said she didn't care and my father turned his head back toward her to really let loose when we felt

BUMP and heard a scream and this woman came out of her house like she'd been shot out of a cannon, screaming, "Oh NO! Oh NO! You've run over BENNY!"

"Oh, good God!" shouted my father, jamming on the brakes, which only meant we stayed directly on top of poor Benny. "Oh my GOD! I didn't see. I was looking in the backseat. Oh my GOD!"

The woman was crying and carrying on, as you might expect. My mom and Mag leaped out of the car and my mom said, "Oh, poor, poor little pussy."

And that's how my father found out he'd run over a cat. He thought he'd run over the woman's child. Not that running over someone's cat wasn't horrible, but it shows you how relative things can be.

"Never give an animal a human name," he said to me later. "Never." He usually elaborated more on his good advice, but he was a little terse after the whole incident, as you can imagine.

My father got out of the car. Then the woman did this amazing thing. She went and put her arm around my father and said, "You poor man. You must feel terrible." We all looked at her like she was from the moon, which I suppose in a way she might as well have been, Kansas being such a foreign place to us. And she invited us all to sit on her porch and have a cool drink. She was still crying, and she kept her arm around my dad as she shepherded him toward the porch, and I hope I was the only one who saw him flinch when some of her wet tears that she wiped on her arm touched *his* arm. You know, you'd like to think you'd be saintly or even unusually kind in such circumstances, but I guess some stranger's secretions are still going to gross you out.

The woman went into the house, first disengaging my father, then she came back out with a garbage bag and asked my father if he would mind. At first I think he thought she wanted him to take out the garbage because he looked kind of confused, and then he got it and went back to move the car off dead Benny. After he had the thing bagged he didn't seem to know what to do with it. He couldn't just put it in the woman's garbage. Mag took a branch and kind of scraped the guck off the road and threw it in a ditch when the woman had gone back in the house to get some refreshments for us, and finally my father put the bag in the trunk of our car and then knocked on the woman's door and asked her if she wanted the remains and she looked around like maybe they had a spare urn lying handy or something and finally said no, and then asked us if we'd like to stay for dinner.

Well, nobody really wanted to stay, but it was late in the day and we were hungry and also at that moment her husband was heading in from the fields and the woman went running out to him and we all braced ourselves in case he didn't take it quite as well as she did, but he came on the porch and said, "Sandy says she's sorry, she forgot to introduce herself. My wife is Sandy Schultz and I'm Bud. She's just gone in to get some pork chops out of the freezer for dinner. Now, you all stay and we're not taking no."

My father stood up and shook his hand first, then my mom and Mag, and finally me, and my hand disappeared in his, which was the size of a catcher's mitt, and we told him our names and I had a funny thought that I was glad my name was something ordinary and midwest like Henry and not one of those weird names boys get sometimes like a boy in my class named Ashton. I would not want to be introduced as Ashton to this man, although it was clear he would be nice about it. They both would be. They were the nicest people I'd ever met.

Then their children, Marla and Jim, came home. They were teens and as far from Puppy and Nadine as you could get. They were clearly all cut up about the cat, but they took me off to the barn to see the other animals and asked all about my life in Virginia. Then we came back and washed our hands and everyone sat in the living room and ate cheez doozies, which were Sandy's specialty, kind of like a bread stick with cheese in it, and my mom went to help Sandy in the kitchen.

My father tried to fold himself into an inconspicuous shape on the sofa. I could hear my mother in the kitchen, kind of trying to explain away the accident by saying my father had been really sick with malaria.

"Oh, poor poor man," said Sandy. Later, when Bud emerged all washed up and gleaming red from scrubbing off the dirt, she told him that my parents had just been to Africa.

"No kidding. Africa," said Bud. "No kidding." Like it was the most amazing thing that had ever happened to anyone on a farm in Kansas: a man who'd just been to Africa driving through and killing their cat. Would wonders never cease? I think it almost made my father proud, the little bit of exotica he had brought to these people's lives and it never would have happened if he hadn't killed their cat. So in a way . . . You could see just by watching his face that that was the way he was trying to work it out.

"Now, if you're looking for something fun to do locally, there's an ice cream museum north of Omaha we used to take the kids to. That was fun, wasn't it, kids?"

"Oh, you'll love it," said Marla.

"Great ice cream, too!" said Jim.

The whole family was like that, totally weird about their pet's demise. Nobody said a mean word to any of us about it.

My dad tried to apologize again at dinner, but Sandy just passed him the whipped candied sweet potatoes and said, "Now, you just stop that, Norman. Everyone knows that nobody in their right mind would run over a cat on purpose. It's just one of those things that happens. My goodness, it's not like it's the first animal that's ever died."

"Gosh, yes, you must feel awful," said Marla. "Have a Parker House roll."

"It must have been a shock, the, uh, crunch," agreed Jim, and they both looked at us in so friendly and kindly a manner that it might have been creepy but it wasn't like, say, born-again Christians with that kind of frightening gleam. They were just nice people, is all. So we settled down to a really good dinner and Bud told us the story of their horse.

"We haven't always had this big spread. Belonged to my dad and was kind of understood I'd take it over when he died, but in the meantime we had just a little hobby farm, just two acres on a dead end with a bunch of other two-acre properties, and we had a horse that no one rode, just a pet really, but we were real fond of it, and the only place to keep it was the front yard, because most of the property was in front of the house, but we were worried the neighbors wouldn't like it. No one else had an animal, and the manure and all. But everyone loved that horse, especially Mrs. Grady, who lived at the end of the street. We didn't even know Mrs. Grady until we got the horse. She and her husband were paramedics and worked odd hours, kept to themselves, and their house was hidden behind trees. But then one day we saw Mrs. Grady feeding the horse apples, and Marla, who took care of the horse, stopped to talk to her. Seemed she bought an entire bushel of apples just for the horse and would stop to and from work every day to feed and pet him. She just oozy-oozied over him. Well, she was childless and we were glad she got some satisfaction from it because it turned out her husband had cancer. They weren't old, about forty-five, fifty, wouldn't you say?"

" 'Bout that," said Sandy, busy passing the Jell-O salad and the pickled beets and the potato salad and the macaroni salad. Seems like anything these people had, you throw it in with a little mayonnaise and you got yourself a salad.

"So it was really sad to think of this woman being left childless and husbandless; we began to think we should just *give* her the horse and be done with it."

"Except we were real fond of it ourselves," said Jim.

"Especially me," said Marla. "It was really my horse."

"Well now, Marla," said Bud.

"In spirit it was," said Marla.

"Well, perhaps," said Bud. "Now, this woman, Mrs. Grady, she really loved the horse, too, but darned if she didn't start feeding it the queerest things. Started out with apples and carrots."

"Nothing queer about that," said Jim.

"Heck no," said Bud. "Nor sugar cubes, and I've seen people give horses a lick from their ice cream cones."

"And then eat the rest themselves. I've seen that," said Sandy. "Seen them do it with their dogs, too. Isn't that just the thing now, Katherine, isn't it?"

My mom nodded.

"All that's okay. To be expected. But then one day we go out and we find this pile, this pile of this *stuff* on the ground, and the horse lapping it up, and I go, 'Jim, what's this stuff?' " said Bud.

"And I go, 'I dunno,' " said Jim.

"And I say, 'Looks like spaghetti to me,' " said Bud.

"And I go, 'Me too,' I'll never forget that. I just go, 'Me too.' Don't I, Dad?" said Jim.

"That's what you went, 'Me too.' Well, like two idiots we watch that horse eat the spaghetti until it's gone, even knowing it's no good for him. And we knew, sure as shooting, where it came from," said Bud.

"We were kind of like, what you might call, in shock, I guess, 'cause we let that horse eat the spaghetti before we thought to stop it. We knew it was Mrs. Grady gave it to him because we'd just seen her stop her car there as she did every day on the way to work."

"We thought she was giving him *sugar* cubes. Or apples. Carrots and the like," said Bud.

"Same as always."

"That's why we were too shocked by the spaghetti to do anything and then darn if the poor horse didn't have colic all night. Had to call the vet, and he said, 'What's this horse been eating anyhow?' and Jim says, 'Spaghetti,' and he says, 'Well sir, you can't give spaghetti to a horse,' and we say, 'We know that. We're fixin' to say somethin' to the lady who gave it to him.' 'Now, that wouldn't be your wife, would it?' asks the vet, 'because I always thought she was a *sensible* lady.' And we say, 'No sir, it would not.' And he says, 'Well, what lady would it be, then?' And we say, 'Lady down the street. Name of Mrs. Grady.' As if her name made any difference. And he scratches his head and says, 'Well, Bud, guess you better go talk to this Mrs. Grady.' And I say, 'I been fixin' to do that.' And when he leaves we go down the street and knock on Mrs. Grady's door and tell her no more spaghetti for the horse and she looks kind of put out like we don't appreciate the favor she done us but goes, okay, no more spaghetti. So the next day we see her car pull up on the way to work, same as always, and we see her drop something from a bucket onto the ground and the horse is eating it, so we go over to have a look-see and it weren't spaghetti, were it, Jim?"

"No, it weren't," said Jim. "It surely weren't."

"Well, what were, uh, was it?" asked my mother, who was getting into the story big time, I could tell.

"It was french fries," said Jim.

"Now, can a horse eat those?" asked my mom.

"No, Katherine, they sure can't," said Bud. "You're right on the mark about that. They sure can't. And the thing of it was, I thought Mrs. Grady could kind of ex-trapolate, you know. About the spaghetti. Figuring like, no spaghetti, then no french fries either."

"But it seemed like she could not," said Jim.

"So it seemed. Wasn't much for extrapolation," said Bud. "So we had to go back. Speak to her again. 'Carrots and apples,' we said to her, 'carrots and apples.' But it didn't take. The next time it was baked ziti. I had to speak to her sternly after that. And I don't like to be stern."

"No, you sure don't," said Sandy.

"But he had to because I was so upset," said Marla.

"Well, we all were," said Sandy. "Poor horse."

"But especially me," said Marla.

"You were, poor dear," said Sandy, tsking.

"I said, 'Now listen, Mrs. Grady, if you can't stick to the fruit and vegetable line of things, we're going to have to ask you, much as we hate to, you with your husband's cancer and all, to quit feeding our horse,' " said Bud, scratching his head. "I felt real bad about that."

"We all did," said Sandy.

"I probably felt least bad," said Marla.

"And Mrs. Grady did, God bless her, she stopped with the spaghetti and french fries and baked ziti and marsh-mallows and stuff. The next thing we found dumped there was pineapple and star fruit. 'Mrs. Grady!' I said when we came over to see what she'd dumped. 'It's fruit,' she said defiantly. 'You said fruit and vegetables. Well, I gave him fruit.' And that's the night the horse died," said Bud.

"It was fruit that killed the horse," said Jim. "Exotic fruit. Tropical fruit."

" 'Not my fault. You said fruit was okay,' Mrs. Grady said when we informed her the horse was dead. 'I certainly did,' I said. She had me there. I'd said fruit," said Bud.

"Stressed, the woman was under a lot of stress," said Sandy, passing the potatoes and butter around again.

"Yep," said Bud. "Maybe a little indifferently depraved, as they say on *Law and Order*. On a bad day. Being under all that pressure. Dealing with all that cancer like she was."

"Couldn't have been easy," said Marla.

"They had a big vegetable garden," said Jim. "More than they could eat."

"But I guess they thought the horse would prefer spaghetti," said Marla.

"Well, everyone likes pasta," said Sandy.

"Tell you the truth, her baked ziti looked pretty good," said Bud.

"And she could grow gentians like nobody's business. We didn't really blame them for the death of the horse, now, did we?" said Sandy.

"I don't know if you can ever really blame anyone for the death of a horse, now, can you?" asked Bud, and I wanted to stand up and scream, "YES! YES, you can blame someone for the death of a horse or running over a cat, or any number of things. What is the matter with you people?" But they seemed to have us under a spell, the same kind they were under, because I knew under normal circumstances Mag would have made short work of such a provocative question. And it occurred to me that maybe we're not meant to get along, like maybe someone took a wrong turn in even thinking that should be anyone's goal. That in bouncing off each other we get to see stuff. These people were having a picnic without the ants and I found myself missing the ants. Although I could see it was just their way and I wouldn't have missed seeing it, it was so weird.

"Naw. Not in the end. They were under a lot of stress," said Bud.

"A *lot* of stress. Well now, who's for some ambrosia?" asked Sandy, getting up to get a fruit concoction topped with lots of whipped cream and mini marshmallows. And then Sandy took my mom out to show her her gentians. She had spectacular gentians that year and she felt sure my mother would appreciate them, and because the rest of us didn't know what to do, we followed right along, and they were swell gentians all right. And then Sandy asked my mom how gardening was in Virginia and what did she think of painting the parlor a gentian blue to go with her gentians, and my mother said her walls were all white (Mag and I looked at each other but didn't say anything), but when she got home maybe she'd paint them gentian blue to remember this day. Except for your poor cat, she blurted out quickly when she remembered the day might not have been completely perfect as far as the Schultzes were concerned.

"Well, we've had a swell time, too," said Sandy. "Your stopping by has been a blessing, and Benny probably had just run through all nine of his lives. No matter how many lives you've got, you have to run through them all eventually."

"I think *everyone* should paint their parlor walls gentian blue," gushed my mother.

"Don't you worry none," said Bud, patting my dad's arm and then giving it a little sock that you could tell was going to leave a bruise although he didn't mean it; he was just a big guy. "That malaria, I hear it can really get you down."

And hearing it that way it was as if none of us had really considered that before.

"Can I make you some sandwiches for the road?" called Sandy, but we had already pulled away, leaving the Schultzes waving in the sunset.

We drove a couple miles down the road in silence.

"Cat killer!" said Mag.

And for a while after that nobody said anything.

Welcome to Iowa

YOU'D THINK that such a display of rampant forgiveness would inspire others to go and do likewise, and I waited hopefully, but it didn't seem to have any effect on anyone. There was a kind of resolved quiet in the car. Nobody argued anymore or acted overtly unpleasant, but it wasn't the cheery camaraderie of days of old either. We rode a long way before anyone remembered we had a dead cat in the trunk of the car and everyone had a different idea about whose fault *that* was, too. We were headed for the Ice Cream Capital of the Universe Museum as per the Schultzes' suggestion. This looked to be fun, and as we talked about it over breakfast it would have been nice to think that this day would be a great trip day, but my dad was eating breakfast alone with me. Mag and my mom were at another table with their backs to us. I kept going back and forth between the two tables. It was then that I hit a kind of despair. I was mad at both of them for making this trouble because neither one of them would budge.

"It says here in the brochure, son, that they make fifty kinds of ice cream, including several in unusual colors, and that they have, apart from the museum, a theater and a 1920s nostalgic ice cream parlor."

"Mmm," I said, eating my toast without enthusiasm.

My father must have sensed this because he was working hard to cheer me up without doing the thing that would have actually worked, making up with my mother. I was frustrated because I could see how each of them was screwing things up but I couldn't get them to see it. I was expending a lot of energy trying to make things how they should be and thinking I could only hum and put out rosette soaps when I got my ducks in a row, and when everyone finally behaved, *then* I could have that kind of humming energy Liesl had. And that's why I was so annoyed, because they weren't cooperating. I hated the tension between them so much that I could hardly stand to be with them. It was okay when Pigg and Mag fought, but this was my mom and dad. This really *mattered*. How could they not see this? How could they do this to me? How could they do it to the three of us? Why couldn't they try to see each other's point of view, even when I tried to explain it to each of them?

I was staring at the table in a funk thinking about this when my dad said, "Penny for your thoughts," and I said truthfully that I was thinking about Liesl and how she was humming and putting out rosette soaps when she practically didn't know us, and my dad said how that seemed a mistake to him, how she should have waited to see how things panned out with Cody and Pigg, or if we all turned out to be thieves or ax murderers or something, and how it would have been even more appropriate to wait until he and Mom came for the wedding and the family had assembled, but I thought no . . . NO. What I liked was how she hummed and put out the rosette soaps right then. It didn't matter what *we* did, all the humming and putting out of the soaps was coming from her. And how different that was from the people whose cat we killed. How they scurried around to make things okay even when they weren't. It didn't seem to me that Liesl did that. She didn't seem to have an idea of how things were supposed to be. But those people whose cat we killed had an idea of how things were supposed to be and were working overtime to make them that way, just like I was working overtime to force my parents to make up so everything would be okay. And that seemed to me to be the difference between them and Liesl, or me and Liesl for that matter. They were all, Liesl and the cat people, nice folks and wanted to like you, but the cat people thought they had to make everything okay so that they could like you, which they wanted to do, but they had to fix up circumstances or you first, so they scurried to do that, but Liesl had changed herself in some profound way so that the okay part somehow came instead from inside her and the outside circumstances didn't matter at all. And then I could see that nothing from the outside had to change the way I was. And if I wasn't dependent on outside things, I didn't have to change them either. I could let them be.

And so we returned to the car and rode along toward the ice cream museum in a kind of resigned quiet. The general tone of the car was neither happy nor unhappy. My mother was driving and Mag napped and my father stared out the window with a sort of grudge-holding look, but I was feeling, I don't know, luminous almost, kind of free.

When we got there, the ice cream museum was terrific. It was a small museum, which is my favorite kind. The kind of museum I like is the kind you can knock off in five, ten minutes flat. They had plenty of postcards and ice cream souvenirs in the gift shop and the admission fee was only fifty cents, which made both my dad and Mag very happy. I don't think my mother ever thought much about money one way or the other, so this couldn't be a source of happiness for her, and I felt a bit sorry for her about that.

Then the most splendid thing happened: we were eating in the old-fashioned ice cream parlor, the only people there at eleven o'clock in the morning, and were about halfway though our large multicolored ice creams, multicolored being the most interesting feature of their ice cream, the flavors being rather ordinary, of the butter pecan and coconut pie type, nothing you haven't seen a million times before, and a few men and a woman walked in, all in baseball uniforms, and they said to the girl who made our ice creams for us, "Bessie, you get your butt out from behind that counter, we got six team members not showing up for the game and we're going to have to forfeit if you don't." And Bessie said, "Aw, come on, guys, you know I can't leave the soda fountain. What if a customer comes? I'll get fired."

"Who's going to fire you? Your grandpa? He's out there waiting for us to get a team together PDQ so we don't lose the whole tournament."

"He say to get me?" asked Bessie. "Did he say get ole Bessie and never mind who's minding the store?"

And the men all hemmed and hawed and the woman said, "Come on, Bessie, we need some estrogen on the team."

"Can't do yer and you know it."

And then the man turned to us and said, "What about you folks? Ever play any baseball?"

And the miracle was all of us had. At one time or another, but I expected my mom and Mag and my dad all to say "No," and "You've got to be kidding," and "We've got to make time to Indiana," and stuff, but instead my malaria-ridden dad surprised me and said, "Well, I'm game." And then I said, "Me too," and my mom and Mag said, "Well, why not?" And the man said, "Suit 'em up, Buford," and Buford took us to a shed behind the ice cream parlor and found us all uniforms. They fit more or less except for mine, which was too big, so I just wore the jersey. We never really learned anyone's name, although they did introduce us. They managed to get two other players from the parking lot and we went out on the field behind the museum where the stands were full of on-lookers from I don't know where. It turned out to be four teams from four local dairies that played each other every week, the dairy owners being rivals to the death. The owners were all fat older guys, red in the face from shout-ing themselves hoarse at their players. One of them called one of his workers/team players a bandy-legged left-footed pussy willow, but she didn't take offense, just waved her hand at him to shut up, she was trying to de-cide whether to steal home. It was a tournament, so after every game we changed fields, but because everyone was complaining that their pickup players weren't as good as another team's, they kept rotating us as well, so that sometimes I was playing with my mom and sometimes with Mag and sometimes all four of us were on the same team. My mom was an okay hitter and could run, but she couldn't catch for beans. Mag was just all-round hopeless, which no one mentioned to her, but I noticed that whenever she went up to bat the dairy owner slapped his forehead in despair. My dad was great. And I wasn't bad myself. I didn't know how good until we played that foreign competition. And there was ice cream. Ice cream everywhere, in the dugout, in center field, people constantly walking around with little paper cups of the stuff for you to refresh yourself. I've never seen anything like it. And we played ball all day under that hot Nebraska sun.

Finally, of course, it all had to end, and we made our way back to the shed by the museum to turn in our uniforms, all grass-stained, dirty, and exhausted. The dairy people slapped us on the backs and thanked us. Then we got back in the car.

Nobody said anything. We were still glowing from the unexpected baseball, from the long perfect summer day and all that ice cream. There was a dreamy twilight haze as the sun lowered toward the cornfields, as if the air had trapped the light and thickened with it. There was nothing making noise for miles but the peaceful buzz of crickets and the sound of our car parting the stillness. I don't know. I don't know. How can you not love it all?

And then we drove endlessly, endlessly over the gentle crests. A sign said: Welcome to Iowa.

Go Fish!

GOFISH

POLLY HORVATH

What did you want to be when you grew up?
I wanted to be a writer, a dancer, and a nun.

What was your worst subject in school?
Math. When I got to geometry in tenth grade, it made me weep.

Where do you write your books?
I have an office in our basement. It's very private with a window overlooking a lot of fruit trees where the horse likes to graze. He snorts, I write. Sometimes, I snort. I don't know if he writes.

Which of your characters is most like you?
Uncle Martin in *The Corps of the Bare-Boned Plane*.

Are you a morning person or a night owl?
I'm a morning person. When I'm doing a first draft, I have to work in the morning.

What's your idea of the best meal ever?
Cheese and crackers, and red wine. Or lobster and clams at a lobster pound in Maine. Or a cruiser day lunch, which only people who have gone to Camp Nebagamon will understand.

Which do you like better: cats or dogs?
Dogs. I love dogs. I could never live without a dog.

What do you value most in your friends?
Tolerance and finding the same things funny that I do.

Where do you go for peace and quiet?
We live in miles of wilderness on our doorstep, so generally, I just go outdoors.

What's your favorite song?
"Hallelujah" by Leonard Cohen, sung by Rufus Wainright.

Who is your favorite fictional character?
Jo March or anyone from *Sweet Thursday* by John Steinbeck, which is my favorite book.

What are you most afraid of?
Something happening to the people I love.

What time of the year do you like best?
Autumn, around Halloween, when everything is golden.

If you were stranded on a desert island, who would you want for company?
My husband, daughters, our dog, and our horse. Then I wouldn't be stranded.

SQUARE FISH

In a brilliant, hilarious, and delightfully crass story,
the incomparable Polly Horvath tells the story of 13-year-old Ratchet,
and her summer in Maine with her eccentric great-aunts, hearing
strange stories from the past and encountering
a variety of unusual and colorful characters.

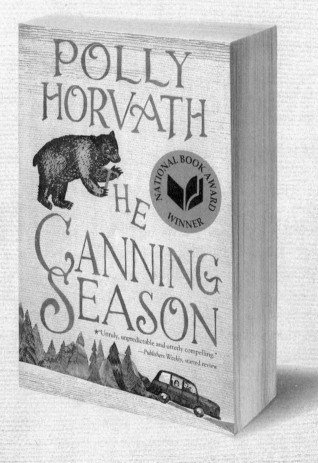

Keep reading for a sneak peek of *The Canning Season*.

MRS. MENUTO LOSES HER HEAD

"I'm going where?" Ratchet gasped.

"Maine."

"Maine?" Ratchet cried. "Why am I going there?"

"You're spending the summer with great–second cousins, Tilly and Penpen Menuto. You can just call them aunts. I called them Aunt Tilly and Aunt Penpen, and they always referred to me as their niece. You can be a niece, too. Who says 'Great–second cousin once removed Tilly' or whatever it would be. It's too much of a mouthful. They're some distant relatives or other. I'd almost forgotten about them. I used to spend summers with them. You're old enough now to get some away-from-home experience, and that's the only free place I could think of."

"I'm going tonight? Why didn't you tell me before?"

"I thought it would make a nice surprise. Come on, hurry up, it's going to take two days to get there. I've got train and bus tickets for you. You'll like sleeping on the train. The clickety-clack and all that. Here's your itinerary. Hurry up, Ratchet, get your coat."

"But it's hot out," Ratchet said.

"Not in Maine. Don't they teach you anything in school?" Henriette was walking swiftly up the basement stairs to the parking lot. She drove purposefully with no idea where she was going. She had never been to the train station, but she figured, what the heck, she had a map. Henriette took the same routes through Pensacola and never deviated from her habitual courses. Within minutes they were lost. Ratchet clutched her seat nervously as Henriette, flustered that the streets weren't where she figured they should be, almost hit a pedestrian and ran a stop sign. It was at this point that Henriette remembered Ratchet's suitcase sitting at home.

"Too late," she said. "Too late. Damn it. Well, I'll try to remember to send you a few things." She swung into a convenience store to find someone who could tell them how to get to the train station, and they got there just minutes before the train pulled out.

"I didn't even know I *had* any relatives," Ratchet said as they hurried across the platform.

"They were already old when I spent summers with them. They must be casket-ready by now. Penpen was kind of fat and happy-happy all the time, and Tilly looked like a sphincter."

"Like a what?" Ratchet asked, but the conductor was hurrying her up the steps to the train. She and her mother didn't say good-bye. Her mother had long ago told her that in their family they were no good at hellos, no good at goodbyes, and not much good with the stuff in between. As Ratchet turned, she could hear her mother trying to shout something to her over the roar of the train starting up.

"What?" Ratchet called through the open train door.

"Keep That Thing covered!" Henriette cried and headed back to the parking lot.

Ratchet watched her mother's retreating form as long as she could, then went into the train car. People were already slumped and slumbering, their faces pressed against windows, or their heads hanging heavy on their chests. There weren't any seats next to women available, so she sat next to a man who was sound asleep and drooling slightly on his lapel. She felt a terrible wrench at being pulled away from her mother, like a boot being pulled out of thick mud with a great sucking sound. But she knew her mother would despise such feelings. They were fussy. She put her feet and knees together and her hands in her lap and kept this position pretty much all the way to Maine.

Tilly was tiny and very, very thin. Penpen was round and jolly, just as Henriette had said, and even though she had short white hair, she didn't look all that old. Not nearly as old as Tilly, but Ratchet knew that she must be because the first thing that Tilly said to her when she got in their waiting car was, "We are twins. We were born together, we grew up together, we have lived our whole lives together, and we have plans to die together. The thing is, as I tried to explain to your mother, who by the way—"

"We are living somewhere very remote," interrupted Penpen, flashing Ratchet a smile from the front seat.

"So if we die, you will be stuck, that's all I was trying to tell Henriette! But, as usual, she wasn't listening. Stuck," said Tilly glumly, putting on her driving gloves.

Tilly sat on two phone books and a cushion and yet she could barely see over the wheel. Ratchet sat in the backseat. It was black out. In fact, the night sky, the whole night air of the Maine woods, had an oily quality—a dark so deep you could almost see rainbows in it. Ratchet had no idea where she was. Her ticket said "Dairy," but Henriette had told her that her great-aunts had a house past Dink. All these "D" names blurred in her mind as they drove through tiny lit streets. Finally even the few lights of town were gone and she was too tired to track their journey further. Too tired to do anything but try to remain upright in the backseat and be polite.

"If something were to happen to one of us, as I *tried* to explain to your mother on the phone, you'd be sunk," Tilly went on.

"Unless you learn to drive the Daimler, of course."

"Your mother—"

"Oh, look, a bear!" said Penpen.

Ratchet pressed her face to the window to see the bear but saw nothing except more darkness, so she leaned back. The roads became narrower. Penpen asked if anyone wanted a brown bag, of which they kept a healthy supply up front "just in case." Ratchet reached a hand forward for one, but although Tilly's driving made her queasy she never needed to use it. Instead she fidgeted, twisting and untwisting it. Tilly drove twenty miles an hour and made many sudden jerky stops because she kept thinking she saw things in the dark. Penpen would crane her neck around, checking the car on all sides, before saying, "Drive on, Tilly." And Tilly would drive on until she saw the next mirage and jerked to another stop, and another, until they finally stopped for good beyond a gate with a sign reading GLEN ROSA.

The Menuto house was enormous, made from old brick and spouting a profusion of towers and turrets that reached up in line with the tops of the pines that encircled it to prick the vast starry sky. From the front yard, where Tilly stopped the car, Ratchet could hear the sound of the sea crashing on rocks somewhere below. She tripped sleepily toward the house. She had spent forty-eight hours traveling, most of them sleepless, and could barely keep track of her feet.

"Don't fall down the cliff," said Penpen, grabbing Ratchet's shirt between her shoulder blades and yanking her back. Ratchet was so tired that the sudden sight of white foam spraying below and the realization that she had almost joined it with a splash didn't startle her, but Penpen's hand on her shirt did. She immediately and instinctively jerked away, wondering if Penpen had felt That Thing through the thin fabric. But if she had, she registered nothing. Ratchet looked down after that and followed the white rock walkway up to the house. She was too tired to take any notice of her surroundings. All she could remember as she drifted off to sleep was climbing a large winding staircase and being shown to a room from where she could hear the sound of the sea even louder, banging its way toward shore and back. Why does it keep doing that? she thought; why can't it just shut up? and fell asleep in her underwear.

———

"The most immediate concern," said Tilly the next morning over waffles with raspberries—there seemed to be a great deal of raspberries around; there were baskets of them rotting all over the house—"is clothes. Most specifically, but not entirely, Penpen, summer clothes."

"Swimsuit," said Penpen.

"Shorts."

Underwear, thought Ratchet.

"She hasn't even a toothbrush!" said Tilly indignantly. "Her mother—"

"*Would* you like some more berries?" interrupted Penpen, passing a large bowl across the table to Ratchet.

"How did you sleep?" asked Tilly.

"Good," said Ratchet. It was the deepest sleep she could remember ever having. She had never slept above ground in an upstairs bedroom. There were no underground insects drilling small holes. She had awakened groggily in the middle of the night to see the wind off the ocean fluttering the yellow dotted-swiss curtains in front of her octagonal window. I have a porthole, she thought. She wanted to call Henriette and tell her. Ratchet tried to stay awake to watch the fluttering curtains in the light of a moon that emerged in the middle of the night, but she was too tired. Sometime during her sleep she had surrendered to the sound of the surf, the soothing waves, their deep rhythm creeping into her unconscious all night like the heartbeat of a large animal.

"Go out and get some air," said Penpen. "Tilly and I must tidy up and get our hats and then we will go make the necessary purchases in town."

Ratchet went outside to explore. The morning was bright, sunshine sparkling on the water, filtering through the pine trees. She didn't bother to put on her shoes but scrambled down the rocky edge of the cliff to dangle her feet in the sea. A seal swam by and a fishing boat chugged along in the distance. Sea gulls made a great deal of early-morning mindless noise. But it was all strange sounds, strange sights. These were not Florida gulls, they were strange northern gulls. Even with the porthole she did not want to be here and wondered if she would be able to keep her breakfast down.

"Come along," shouted Tilly from the cliff top. Ratchet ran up the cliff for her shoes.

"We're going into Dink, dear," said Penpen.

They climbed into the Daimler. Penpen, with a grimly sympathetic look, gave Ratchet a brown bag. Tilly still drove with a series of slow violent jerks, as if the car itself were heaving its way down the road, but Ratchet was distracted by seeing the countryside she hadn't been able to see the night before. First the dirt road ran inland through thick bushes that scratched against both sides of the Daimler. Then it widened and swampland appeared, and woods so deep it looked as if night had fallen permanently beneath them. Blueberry bushes grew everywhere in the swamps, and in the distance she saw a large animal drinking.

"Oh, look at the moose, Tilly!" said Penpen, which caused Tilly to drive off the road into a bush and it took fifteen minutes to maneuver the car back onto the road.

"Please do not point out any more wildlife, Penpen," said Tilly. "If we get stuck here, we'll be stuck forever. None of us could walk all the way to town."

"I'm almost certain Ratchet could. You have good strong legs, don't you, Ratchet?" asked Penpen.

"I don't know," Ratchet said, looking down uncertainly at them. When Henriette saw them she always said, "There's your father's bony knees staring at me like a reproach."

"Even if she could walk it, it would only be to be eaten by a bear along the way," said Tilly.

"True, too true," said Penpen.

"There was that incident years ago."

"But that was *many* years ago," said Penpen.

"Yes," said Tilly and sighed as if the subject were closed. "You see, Ratchet, that's what I meant when I said that if we were to die and you were alone at Glen Rosa . . ."

"And could not drive . . ."

"And could not walk . . ."

"You'd be pretty much sunk."

"What about the telephone?" Ratchet asked.

"You can't call out, you can only get calls in," said Tilly. "Father fixed it that way the year after we first got the phone. It was because our mother developed a habit."

"She certainly did," said Penpen.

"She phoned everyone."

"The San Diego Zoo, people in China, proprietors of shops in Little Rock, Arkansas. She had this great curiosity about the world. It was a wonderful thing, really."

"And if Father had only let her travel I'm sure she would never have developed the habit. But he kept her here on our property, far from anything, and didn't even let her do the shopping."

"He thought it was undignified. A Menuto shopping! That's what servants were for."

"So she never got to go anywhere or meet anyone. It was a real tragedy."

"She's what people today would have called a people person," said Penpen.

"So at least she was spared that," said Tilly, "dying when she did. At such an early age."

"We were just girls, Tilly and I. Exactly your age, actually."

"How did she die?" Ratchet asked.

"She offed herself," said Penpen.

"What?" Ratchet said.

"She killed herself in a particularly brutish and horrible way. I don't know why. I suppose it was all she could come up with at the time. Or maybe she was experimenting. She was very imaginative."

"How did she do it?" Ratchet asked.

"She cut off her own head."

"Oh no!" said Ratchet.

"I suppose you think that's rather thrilling," said Penpen. "People think children are going to be upset by things that I'm sure they think are quite thrilling. Tilly and I were proud of her. It must have taken extreme nerve, wouldn't you say, Tilly?"

"It wasn't your ordinary way to go. Mother never did anything the ordinary way."

"Weren't you so sad?" asked Ratchet.

"Oh, we were," said Penpen, "for many many years. She was a wonderful woman, but she simply wasn't made to be closeted up like that. Anyhow, Father never bothered changing the phone line afterward. I guess he thought it would come in handy when we had swains. Not that things ever became very swainish around our house. Too far out. And so Tilly and I just kind of stayed on, and then when we were in our teens Father died. We dismissed the servants after that and buried Father in the backyard, and Tilly and I taught ourselves to drive."

"We never bothered with silly things like licenses," said Tilly. "At the time you didn't need them."

"No, but it doesn't matter, of course," said Penpen.

"All these things that people 'out there' think you need that are complete hogwash. Anyhow, I reminded your mother when she phoned that we were in a very remote area and could really not take on the responsibility of a child. Not because we couldn't care for one but because we plan to die together, and if we suddenly do, then you'd be trapped out here. It isn't a pretty thought. But Penpen had to go and become a Zen Buddhist."

"Now, now," interrupted Penpen, "I wouldn't go that far. I haven't become anything but interested."

"*She* said," Tilly went on, "that we must take in whatever shows up. You cannot turn anyone away. Take in the whole world, these Buddhists do, if it shows up at their door."

"It's a lovely philosophy, and you see, there you were showing up, just as I was espousing it. Can there be any real accidents? Mustn't we trust in some kind of design to it all?"

"Good thing we don't live closer to town," grumbled Tilly. "We'd be eaten out of house and home. Vacuum cleaner salesmen would be moving in with us. What were those men that used to go door to door selling spices, Penpen? We haven't seen them in years and years. Raleigh men! We'd have Raleigh men in all the spare bedrooms. Just because they showed up at the door. It isn't a practical philosophy."

"I don't believe there are Raleigh men anymore," said Penpen.

"Where did all the Raleigh men go?" asked Tilly.

"And even if there were Raleigh men and even if they showed up, I don't suppose they'd all want to stay."

"Makes no difference, I'm sure you'd be clunking them on the head and dragging them in anyway, Penpen."

"I'm really not like that," Penpen said to Ratchet.

And then they drove quietly, peacefully on.

The trees were opening up over the Daimler and the road widened. Eventually they pulled onto a paved road; then it was still another hour, passing nothing but logging trucks and an occasional lost vacationer, until they came to the small town of Dink, where they bought Ratchet clothes and a few groceries from the general store. The pickings were slim at the store, which was *very* general and seemed to have been stocked randomly—a few nails, a couple of cake mixes, some shower caps, a chicken in a can. Tilly held up the whole canned chicken and she and Penpen burst into hysterical giggles. "Who buys a chicken in a can?" she asked and the two of them snorted, bent double with hilarity as the sullen girl who worked the counter stared at them. They found Ratchet a small woman's swimsuit, which they decided would fit with a few safety pin adjustments. For the rest they had to make do with some boys' clothes that fit Ratchet—some ill-fitting shorts and socks and underwear—and toothbrushes and necessities. Tilly loaded up the counter and paid the girl before moving on to the post office, where they collected six months' worth of mail from their box.

Even though the postmistress knew Penpen and Tilly she made them use their key in the empty postal box before she would go in the back and give them the big bag of mail she had collected for them. "I wish you ladies would come in a mite oftener. The stuff piles up," she said. "Why, you were in town just last week. I saw you. You could have checked your mail then. You ought to get it at least as often as you're in town."

"Nonsense. It's all junk. It does make good tinder in the fireplace," said Tilly and stalked out, dragging a bag of it behind her. "Now let's go get a drink."

Penpen and Tilly took Ratchet through the thick door of the town's tavern, where she was immediately surrounded by unfamiliar smells—it was beer, dampness, cigars, woodsmoke, old wood, and the sweat of many men over many years trapped in the cool dark bar. That was why Tilly and Penpen liked it so much. That was why Ratchet liked it, though none of them knew it. It was the smell of the men. Tilly and Penpen climbed up on stools and ordered glasses of whiskey for themselves and a Coke for Ratchet. They stayed for a long time, eating bar nuts, Tilly drinking many whiskeys and Penpen teaching Ratchet to play pool.

"Well, well, look who's here!" came a voice, and a large man sat down and put his arm around Tilly.

"My goodness, Burl, your stomach is hanging over your pants!" said Tilly.

"Is that any way to speak to your own true love's son?" asked Burl thickly.

"Come on, girls," said Tilly. She threw back the rest of her whiskey. "Time to go home." They spun off their stools and Ratchet made her edgy way around Burl.

"He's drunk," Tilly said tersely as soon as they got outside.

"Who was that?" Ratchet asked as they got in the car.

"Just an old fool," said Tilly, starting the car. "He thinks being born a bastard scarred him for life. As if it made any difference to anyone but him. Myrtle knew it and married him, didn't she? And as if it were my fault! My fault!"

Tilly's driving was even worse on the way home than it had been on the way to town, although Ratchet hadn't thought that possible. Three times they saw a bear coming out of the woods; one of them appeared to be lunging purposefully at the car, veering off at the last second. Ratchet gasped each time one appeared. After the third one ran off, Ratchet caught her breath and said, "They must be *really* hungry."

"I think they only do it to annoy," said Tilly and stepped on the gas, causing the car to lurch suddenly forward and Penpen's head to hit the dashboard. "Goddamn bears."